HER ROGUE MATES

INTERSTELLAR BRIDES® PROGRAM: BOOK 13

GRACE GOODWIN

Published by KSA Publishers
Goodwin, Grace
Her Rogue Mates, Interstellar Brides® Book 12
Cover design copyright 2020 by Grace Goodwin
Images/Photo Credit: Deposit Photos: Angela_Harburn, anasaraholu

Publisher's Note:
This book was written for an adult audience. The book may contain
explicit sexual content. Sexual activities included in this book are strictly
fantasies intended for adults and any activities or risks taken by fictional
characters within the story are neither endorsed nor encouraged by the
author or publisher.

GET A FREE BOOK!

JOIN MY MAILING LIST TO BE THE FIRST TO KNOW OF NEW RELEASES, FREE BOOKS, SPECIAL PRICES AND OTHER AUTHOR GIVEAWAYS.

http://freescifiromance.com

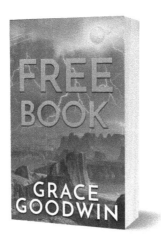

INTERSTELLAR BRIDES® PROGRAM

YOUR mate is out there. Take the test today and discover your perfect match. Are you ready for a sexy alien mate (or two)?

VOLUNTEER NOW!

interstellarbridesprogram.com

1

Harper Barrett, Sector 437, MedRec Transport Station: Zenith, Latiri Star Cluster

DARK HAIR. INTENSE GREEN EYES. THE MAN WHO'D BEEN watching me from the other side of the bar for the last few minutes looked like every woman's wet dream.

Except he wasn't a man. He was an alien.

And this wasn't a bar in downtown Los Angeles, where I grew up. This was Transport Station: Zenith, and every alien warrior in the room was at least six-six, battle hardened and freakishly strong. And those were the small ones.

At five-ten I'd always felt tall. Too tall. Too blonde. Too pretty. Too female to be taken seriously. Men saw me, my blonde hair and D-cups, and assumed I was an idiot. But this alien? He looked mesmerized as he made his way over to me. He didn't stop at the usual "polite" distance. No, he moved in close. Too close.

"I have never seen hair this color," he said, his hand

coming up to brush a wayward lock behind my ear. "It is very beautiful."

I couldn't help but laugh, glancing up at him through my lashes like the proverbial flirt. His teasing *almost* touch hadn't even made contact with my skin, but my heart leapt into my throat anyway.

This was insane. This guy was insane. Insanely hot. He was covered head to toe in some kind of black armor I had never seen before. Definitely not Coalition issue. And the silver band on his arm wasn't familiar either. No officer or ranking insignia. No marker indicating he was part of the Coalition in any way. I knew every race in the Coalition Fleet, had dragged their injured off the battlefield to transport pads, healed them with ReGen wands, held their hands if they were dying. But this guy? He was *different,* and every cell in my body went on high alert.

But the way the other warriors in the room avoided him? The way they watched him almost warily? Like he was a caged tiger? No, not a tiger. A snake. Dangerous. Venomous. I'd seen most of these warriors edgy, ready for battle. And that's how they were acting around him.

Fascinating. But I tried not to show my reaction, or the way my pussy was already hot and aching, my breasts heavy, my pulse pounding. Sheesh. You'd think I hadn't had sex in...forever. Wait. No. I *hadn't* had sex in *forever,* and this guy with his massive shoulders and intense stare was making my body demand I fix that.

Like *now.*

The bartender was a large Atlan female, about six feet tall with breasts the size of melons and stunning dark auburn hair. She was gorgeous. And looking at this guy like she wanted to lick him all over.

Unfortunately, that was a desire I shared.

He smiled at her as she handed him a drink. Her hand lingered on the glass, her fingertips brushing over his in blatant invitation.

I wanted to claw her eyes out.

Shit. I shook my head and turned back to my drink, determined to behave myself. If he wanted the bartender, I didn't blame him. If I were into females, I'd do her, too.

This guy had *trouble* written across his forehead in capital letters. And probably a few more words as well. *Bad boy. Sexy. Eye candy. Rebel. Man whore.* Yeah. Probably a total man whore. He'd probably already slept with half the women on the station.

Been there. Done that. My ex back on Earth had been the cheating kind. Once was enough, thank you very much.

"Why do you frown at me?" he asked, the dark timbre of his voice settling into my bones. A shiver raced over my skin, his voice like a physical caress. My nipples pebbled into hard points, and I had to struggle to breathe normally. Dangerous? Hah! I needed to work on my risk assessment skills. Expand my vocabulary. Dangerous wasn't even close.

"I thought only guys from Earth had horrible pick-up lines," I replied.

"Pick-up lines?"

"Never seen blonde hair? Really? That's the best you can do?"

"I speak the truth." He slowly lowered his head, his dark hair falling rakishly over his forehead.

Did I mention he reminded me of Joe Manganiello? The hottie hunk from *True Blood*? While I assumed this guy wasn't a vampire and had zero intention of biting me, he was working the dark, brooding hero bit. I lifted my glass of what passed for a lager out here in space and indicated a couple of warriors from Prillon Prime who were on the other side of the room. One was brown with amber eyes and dark, rust colored hair. But the other? Golden like a lion. Definitely blond. They were hot, but they didn't make me forget to breathe. Not like this guy was doing. "What do you call that?" I pointed to the fairer warrior.

He crowded closer, dismissing the Prillons with a flicker of movement in his eyes. "They look burned, scorched by the sun. Their skin is thick and ugly." He lifted his hand to the end of my hair where my now ragged ponytail had let loose several rebellious strands. "You are pure light. Soft. Fragile."

I scoffed at that. If he only knew. I was twenty-seven, not seventeen. And I'd been an ER nurse for three years in a busy city hospital before spending almost two years stationed on Transport Station: Zenith being sent off to do battlefield triage and emergency medical service for the Coalition. I was a paramedic in space—which still blew my mind if I really stopped to think about it for too long. But pure? Fragile? Hardly. I tried not to roll my eyes as I turned away from him.

I wasn't pure, but I still had a heart. And after dragging my friend, Henry, out from under a pile of Hive Scouts, looking into what had once been warm brown eyes filled with humor—now dead and cold—that organ was hurting. I really needed more than a beer. Henry Swanson had been born in London. British. From the 22nd SAS. Badass military veteran. Funny accent. Hell of a poker player. Two days ago he'd been smoking cigars, kicking my commander's ass in a game.

Five hours ago, I'd pulled his corpse out from under a stack of dead enemies.

At least he'd taken five of those Hive bastards with him.

Yeah, I needed more than one drink to dull the ache.

Glancing up at the Atlan bartender, I lifted my chin. "Can I get a shot of whiskey, please?"

Her gaze softened, and I realized she really was beautiful. "Sure, honey. Jack, Johnnie, Jim or Glen?"

"Glen."

"Bad out there today?" While her job kept her at the transport station, she knew what we did, the horrors we saw. The lingering emotions.

"Yes."

She nodded and slid a shot glass full of synthesized whiskey toward me. The S-Gen—the matter generator that provided all our clothing, food and other incidentals that came from various planets in the Coalition—on the transport station had been programmed with Jim Beam, Johnnie Walker, Jack Daniels and Glenlivet, as well as a selection of vodkas, gin, beer, wine and every other type of alcohol imaginable from Earth. Drinks I'd never heard of from other planets, too. After puking my guts out in college on tequila, I steered clear of hard liquor most days.

Today was not most days. I just wanted to forget for a while. At least until I was called out on a clean-up mission again.

My mystery alien hottie watched me as I threw back the shot, closed my eyes in bliss as the alcohol burned its way down my throat, and gently placed the shot glass back on the bar like a revered friend.

"You want another one?" the bartender asked.

"No, thanks. We're second wave." We weren't first out,

GRACE GOODWIN

not right now, but we were backup for the next emergency. Which meant I couldn't drown myself in whiskey and pass out in my bed like I wanted to. I fiddled with the band around my wrist, my link to the alert system and the rest of my team. A darker green than my medical uniform, the center of it held a lighted band that communicated orders, coordinates, whatever we might need wherever we were on the ground. But right now, the colored band was a light, airy blue. Baby blue, cotton candy blue. It changed based on status. Red was first call, blue second, and black meant we were considered dormant, off duty. We called it dead time, and it was both rare and valuable.

There were only three emergency medical teams on Zenith, and we were all very, very busy.

"What is second wave?" He stared, like he was putting together a puzzle. Undeterred, he leaned forward when I ignored him, almost as if he was going to...

"Did you just sniff me?" I blurted, leaning back. Our gazes locked, and I felt like a deer in the headlights. I should get up and run, run, run. So why did I freeze in place, almost eager to see what he would do next? I felt like I was dancing with a cobra, and the risk was intoxicating.

"I don't usually need to talk with a female to entice her into my bed." His eyes were pale green, a few shades lighter than mine; my mother always said I had emerald eyes. But his were intense, almost mesmerizing and completely focused on me.

"Yeah, you might be better off with less talking."

He grinned as if I amused him, and his gaze roved over my face, to my lips, then my hair, which he stroked. Involuntarily, I tilted my head into the heated touch. His hand was so big, reminding me of our size difference. I was

6

tall but he was a head taller, if not more. And he was big. No doubt, everywhere. His hand slid down, over my shoulder and lower, to my hand, which he lifted between us. "You are from Earth."

"Yes," I confirmed, although his remark hadn't really been a question. "Never seen an earthling before?" The question dripped sarcasm, but if anything, his smile widened.

"Only one." He didn't elaborate and I didn't ask. I didn't care who he knew or didn't know. Not. My. Business. Besides, if it was a woman, I'd just want to claw her eyes out as well, which was just stupid. What he did and *who* he did it with was none of my business. Better to leave that one alone.

"Why do I smell blood?" He sniffed again, his brows drew together and any bit of playfulness was gone.

I shrugged. Sure, I'd showered and even changed into a fresh uniform, but none of my team had gone to medical to get our bumps and bruises taken care of. As usual, we'd made it back, washed the grime of death away and headed straight for the bar. We were used to losing people, but losing Henry was extra hard. He'd been a practical joker, the comedian and prankster who'd gotten away with murder and made life on this remote station almost fun. Every human on the station had heard of his death by now. Heard, and was heading here to drown their sorrows. In a couple hours, this place would be packed.

Maybe I should have another shot of whiskey. The raucous singing and toasting would go on for hours. I sighed and rubbed my temples. I could feel the headache coming on already.

Sexy alien's eyes narrowed when he saw my hand—the

one he wasn't holding—dark green bandage still in place. "You are hurt."

He switched his grip to the injured one, and I felt small in his hold. The touch was personal, intimate, and made me seem somehow precious. Fussed over. And I found myself hungry for that connection. He was taking liberties, keeping my hand in his as if I belonged to him. He unwound the narrow bandage.

"It's nothing. Really." A small cut on my palm from a piece of ripped metal. I'd had worse while working. Much worse.

He turned my hand palm up, cupped it in one of his and his fingers brushed gently over the gash. It had stopped bleeding before I transported back to Zenith. A scratch. I welcomed the stinging pain. Sometimes, pain was the only way I knew I was still alive. I'd taken a few extra minutes after we transported back, made sure Henry's body got to the morgue and joined my team.

Over hunk's shoulder, I saw our second-in-command, Rovo, watching me. He was with the others, but the look he was giving us gave me pause. He shifted his worried eyes—totally normal expression for Rovo where I was concerned—from me and glared at my companion's back. Hottie must have noticed my distraction and glanced Rovo's way. Their gazes locked for a split second, some kind of alpha male thing going on I didn't understand. But I wasn't worried. I was safe. My entire team was here, sitting along the wall, watching my back, talking trash and unwinding from that shithole, desolate planet we'd just come from.

Fighting over dead planets. While it seemed ridiculous, it made sense. No one wanted a Hive base in this solar system. Hell, this galaxy. So, the Coalition troops fought over dirt. Position. To keep the Hive away.

Space? Earth? Some things didn't change, not when it came to good versus evil. War.

He turned back around, Rovo forgotten. He still held my hand. This was *so* not what I'd expected when I'd made my trip to the bar for a drink. I was supposed to be back with my teammates on the other side of the room, but no. I hadn't moved since he'd invaded my personal space. I hadn't wanted to. Even the cheesy one-liner didn't sway me.

This guy? Holy shit. I wanted to do whatever he wanted. Whatever he said. Right now.

Why? Because I had no doubt he was good. Very, very good. And while I was out here in Sector 437, also known as of the outer quadrant of nowhere, my vagina was becoming as dried up as a Trion desert from neglect. A little male attention felt good.

Especially from one who looked like him. Who stared at me as if he wanted to gobble me right up. Or toss me over his shoulder and lay me down on the nearest horizontal surface—or maybe he'd go for vertical. A wall would do for a quick fix. Hot and hard and rough. A little dangerous? Maybe.

But then, that's what I craved. Something with an edge. Something to make me quiver and gasp and *need*. I didn't want to think right now.

I wanted to feel.

2

Harper

His touch was like a drug, the tingle running through my body all too familiar. Adrenaline junkie? I never denied it. But my fix the past two years usually came from going out on rescue-and-recovery missions for the Interstellar Coalition. More than two hundred and fifty worlds, all with civilizations. Oceans. Storms. Accidents. On Earth, I'd worked as an ER nurse. I'd seen everything from gunshot wounds to decapitations. When the aliens showed up demanding fighters and brides for the Coalition that Earth was now a part of, I was compelled to volunteer. But not as a bride. Forget that. I was no alien brood mare. And I wasn't going to be shooting any kind of gun. I wasn't a fighter; I was a healer. I wanted to have an adventure without domineering mates or fierce battles. To finally see what was out there, in space, on other worlds. *Beam me up, Scotty.*

So I volunteered, told them what I wanted and ended up assigned to this bizarre, alien version of a first responder, paramedic team. The war with the Hive was never ending. Literally. These alien races had been at war with the Hive for centuries. But that didn't mean they never had emergencies. Natural disasters. Surprise attacks. We went in after every battle in this sector of the galaxy and triaged the wounded, helped them survive the aftermath.

Ran from the Hive.

Whatever. It was dangerous, but it made me feel like I was doing something important. Something that mattered and I didn't need to shoot anyone. My team was human, and we followed the human combat units around the Coalition like cheerleaders assigned to a football team. They fought and we went in after. We hung on to the back end of the Battlegroup Karter like leeches. When the commanders moved on, we stayed long enough to clean up the mess. Assuming the Coalition won. If they lost, there was nothing left to save.

The Hive didn't leave raw material behind, and to them, my human brothers and sisters, hell, every single Coalition warrior out there fighting, was meat to be processed.

Most of my MedRec team—Medical Recovery Team— took care of our own the best we could. Sure, a Prillon doctor or Atlan nurse would rush to help a fallen Earth fighter, but something about seeing a human face out here in deep space mattered to the warriors who were lying there bleeding. Dying. Missing home with every breath in their body, afraid they were going to die on the other side of the galaxy.

I lived here now, MedRec Zenith with the rest of my

team. I'd been to more planets and seen more alien races than most in this bar. Yet, I'd never seen anything like *him*.

My mouth watered, and I itched to touch the stubble on his square jaw as he squeezed my hand. I had no idea how long I'd been standing, thinking, staring at him like a mute, but his eyes never left my face. Rovo was completely forgotten. The alien hottie was utterly and completely focused. On me. On the small scratch in the middle of my palm.

"You should have had this healed with a ReGen wand." He didn't wait for me to argue, only pulled one from somewhere on his pants, turned the blue light on and waved it over my palm.

I'd been in space for almost two years, even used the healing wand on the wounded, and I still wasn't used to the healing device. It—along with the more complicated ReGeneration Pod—was miraculous. Within seconds, the wound on my palm knitted closed, turned pink and then disappeared entirely. It had stung before, but I felt nothing now. Numb.

"Thank you," I said once he turned off the wand. While it was polite, it felt wrong somehow. Wrong to walk away without a mark or a scar when the sight of Henry in that transport coffin heading back to Earth still burned the back of my eyelids.

"Why didn't you take care of yourself?" he asked. I noticed a sharper bite to his voice, and I glanced up from our joined hands.

"It was a scratch." I offered him a small shrug and looked up into his eyes. Couldn't look away. I couldn't lie. Didn't want to, so I swallowed and shared my feelings. Yes, feelings.

The things I hid so damn well. "And I needed the whiskey more than I needed a healer."

He slowly shook his head as his thumb slid back and forth over the newly healed flesh. "I am glad I was here then, to tend to you."

So serious. His attention was addictive, the caress making me shiver with delight. I didn't want to pull my hand from his.

Deep shit. That's what this was. Trouble. And I wanted it. I wanted him.

It was time to lighten things back up, to enjoy my break between missions. There wasn't much time for a fling with a mysterious alien man I'd never seen before, and one who'd be gone in a matter of hours, most likely never to be seen again. A fling? No. A quick fuck? Maybe that could work. But I sure as heck didn't want to be in the middle of hot sex with a stranger and have the mission alarms trigger.

Hold that orgasm, dear. I have to go...

There would be no leaving in the middle. Not with this guy. But I really wanted the orgasm—or two—that I knew he'd give me.

He wasn't wearing the uniform of any Coalition branch I recognized. He wore unrelenting black from head to toe—even his hair was as dark as pitch. He had a thick silver stripe around one bicep, but no other variation. Only his eyes held color. Green. He was pale, perhaps even paler than me, which was surprising since I was full-on Nordic blonde, with an Irish dad and mom's family history traced back to Norway. I burned just talking about the sun.

"Lucky me." I gave my coyest smile. I was no expert at flirting, but I wasn't a shy virgin either. This would go nowhere past a quickie. I'd never see him again once the next call came down. So why the hell not? For now, I'd have fun, remember that I was a woman—even in the unisex, bland uniform—and that he was very much a male.

He turned his hand, interlocking our fingers. "Do you have wounds anywhere else?"

"No." Sex-on-a-stick didn't let go of my hand. He was the most amazing specimen of a male I'd ever seen. And I'd been around. Los Angeles was full of man candy, actors and models, surfers and musicians. I came from the land of silicone breasts, Botox and gluteal implants where nothing was real and everyone was gorgeous.

And none of them held a candle to him.

The last two years had been rewarding, and grueling. Most people burned out by the end of their service. I wasn't there yet, but I *was* doing some serious flirting with an alien stranger, so perhaps I was showing signs of stress in a completely different way.

Sex could be a good stress reliever. Especially with Joe Manganiello's alien doppelganger. He'd give me orgasms. Lots of them. Then I could go on my next mission as relaxed and pliable as saltwater taffy.

His gaze dropped and raked over my body, making my nipples harden beneath my bright green uniform. Green meant medical in the Coalition. The docs wore dark, forest green, while we got this lighter version, like emeralds. The color brought out my eyes, I'd been told. There was a thick band of black that hugged the torso. Of course, on the women like me, it only served to highlight the curve of our breasts. I was sure if he wore it instead of his unrelenting black, it would make his chest seem broader. Like that was even possible. He was built like a tank.

He cocked his head to the side and leaned in closer,

inhaling deeply. "I still smell blood, female. I am not sure if I believe you. If you were mine, I would strip you bare and assess every inch of your perfect body to ensure you are completely well."

That made me grin. "You don't believe me?"

"If you were lying, keeping something as important as your health and safety from me, you would not like the consequences."

"Consequences?" My heart leapt at the word. I widened my eyes and waited for him to elaborate. My tongue flicked out to lick my suddenly dry lips.

"Punishment," he said as his eyes followed the motion.

My mouth fell open. I should have been scared. A stranger. An *alien* stranger, wearing a uniform from an unknown planet, was talking about potentially hurting me. Perhaps he was a mind reader because he said, "I do not *hurt* females. I protect them, even, it seems, from themselves. A spanking would certainly remind you that there would be no secrets, that your body was mine to care for, to worship."

Had he just said *spanking*? As in his big, hot hand on my naked backside? Why was that idea so damn hot? I licked my lips again. "You want to worship me?"

His eyes turned darker. While he kept our fingers intertwined, he hooked his other hand about my waist and tugged me closer. "What I will do to you..." He shuddered and leaned in, his breath fanning my neck as his nose brushed over the curve of my ear. We weren't alone; the canteen was at least half full, yet it seemed as if we were in our own little bubble. A bubble where all I could see was him. All I could hear was his deep voice. "Learn every soft curve. I'll find the places that make you catch your breath, that make you shiver with desire. I'll taste your skin. Your pussy. And that's all just the beginning. I will worship you with my mouth."

To say the temperature of the room went way up was an understatement. My uniform was all at once uncomfortable and had too much fabric. I wanted his palm to be touching the bare skin on my back, and preferably moving a few inches lower so he could grab my—

"Do you want to know what I'd do with my fingers?" He pulled back and dipped his chin so our eyes met. Locked. "Or my cock?"

I swallowed. Hard. My mouth watered at the mention of his cock. "Wow, you're really good at this." My voice had a breathy quality I didn't recognize. "My apologies for thinking you had no game."

"What game do you speak of?" he asked, stepping back and tugging me away from the bar. My hand still in his, he pulled me around into a hallway. I let him, abandoning my beer. The hallway was short, with one door at the end lit with a white outline to indicate an emergency exit.

"Picking up women."

With a quick flick of his wrist, my back was against the wall, and he was pressed against me. I felt every hard inch of him and suppressed a moan. My hands were above my head, held in place by his firm but gentle grip. He leaned over me until I was completely immersed in his heat. His free hand came to rest on the curve of my hip, the touch like lightning to my system. I didn't try to get away. I didn't want to. He felt good. Too good.

"I assume that phrase is used on Earth. If I were to pick you up, you would be over my shoulder."

"It means you got me here, alone with you, and I don't

even know your name." Did I just look at his lips? Yes. Yes, I did. And I wanted to know what they felt like against mine, what he tasted like. I looked up to find him watching me intently.

His eyes did that roving thing again, took in my mouth, my neck, my breasts. "You wish to know my name before I kiss you?"

My panties were now ruined. So was my self-control. "Name would be good. Maybe tell me where you're from."

He did the hair tucking thing again and my legs turned to jelly. "My name is Styx. I am part of the Styx legion on Rogue 5."

I frowned. Weird names. "You have a part of a planet named after you?" His finger slid down the side of my neck to rub back and forth across the line of my shoulder. His eyes followed the action.

"Rogue 5 is a moon base. I am the leader of the Styx legion, therefore, the name is mine."

"I've never heard of Rogue 5," I admitted, tilting my head to the side to give him better access.

"It is not part of the Coalition."

That I knew. "Then what are you doing here?"

"I am here meeting a business associate." The way he said the words *business associate* reminded me of a *Sopranos* episode. All that, *Hey, I got a guy...*

"Is everyone from your world as wild as you are?"

He grinned then, his teeth straight and white. "You think me wild?" He shifted his leg so his knee rested between mine, and I was practically riding his thigh.

My mouth fell open, and he took the opportunity to put the tip of his finger on my lower lip. The touch was calloused even as he applied the softest pressure, rubbing back and forth in a delicious tease.

"Tell me your name." Not a request, a demand from an alpha male.

Never one to give in so easily, I leaned forward and took the tip of his finger into my mouth, sucked on it. Once, twice, grazed his skin with my teeth before I released him. Just a little nip, so he'd know I wasn't tamed. "Harper. Harper Barrett from California. I mean Earth."

Great, I sounded like an idiot. But he didn't seem to mind. His pupils were so wide his eyes went almost black, and a vein pulsed in his neck. "I will taste you now, Harper."

Oh. Okay.

I expected slow, but he claimed my mouth with a hunger that made me weak. I couldn't say more, not that I wanted to. I'd flirted, tempted and even taunted a wild, rogue male. He wasn't bound by Coalition rules or consequences. And the way he kissed, with unbridled need and exquisite attention, I knew he did things his own way.

A way I liked very, very much. So did my nipples and my clit and my aching pussy. Yes. I imagined him stripping me right here, filling me with his cock, thrusting into me so hard my back bruised against the hard wall. Yet he was gentlemanly enough to tell me his intentions so I could say no, if I desired. Which I didn't. No, I desired he continue and never stop.

"Something is missing here."

The voice came from my left, and I stiffened because we weren't alone. Styx didn't react. He continued to explore my mouth with a fervor I'd never known before. But it was like I'd been doused in the proverbial bucket of ice water.

I pulled back slightly. "Styx," I murmured, breathing hard.

"Hmm?" he asked, nipping along my jaw.

I turned my head so I could look to the side and Styx took advantage, lowering his mouth to my neck so I couldn't turn away from our visitor. Yes, we were being watched. By a very big, very gorgeous male. He was huge, like Styx, wearing the same uniform. Same silver arm band. But where Styx's hair was shorter and a deep, dark black, this man's hair was actually silver, long and straight and shining. Not gray or blond or any color I'd ever seen before. And his face was chiseled perfection, his eyes a pale gray. He looked like a warrior god from a Dungeons and Dragons fantasy. Not real.

His grin, as his gaze drifted over my body, over Styx's hand locking my wrists above my head, was wicked. And wide.

I twisted my wrists in protest and held myself perfectly still in Styx's arms. Playtime was over. "Styx," I repeated.

He didn't lift his head, just continued to kiss and lick, and even nip along my jaw to my ear, then down my neck. "This is Blade."

Odd introduction, but they obviously knew each other, felt comfortable enough to have a female between them.

"It's...um, nice to meet you," I said, although I wasn't really sure if that was the truth. I twisted harder, and only then did Styx lift his head with a sigh.

"Don't stop for me," Blade said, taking a step closer. "I'll join you." He placed a hand on my cheek, his caress every bit as soul-melting as Styx's had been. Gentle. Awed. And suddenly I felt very...between them.

"Um—"

"Did I mention that Blade and I enjoy sharing a woman between us?" Styx asked.

"Sharing?" I squeaked, my heart pounding so hard I was afraid it would explode. I glanced between the two, their differences like night and day. Salt and pepper. Hot and... hot. Oh. My. God.

"Twice the pleasure for you." Blade's quiet promise sliced through the air with the sharpness of his name. "We will claim a mate together." He leaned down, ran his nose along the side of my cheek and sniffed, just as Styx had done. "Our bite will make you so sensitive, so wild, that the slightest touch will have you coming. Over. And over."

His heated words made me shiver, the hot whisper sliding into my mind like a drug. I was drunk on their attention, my body determined to enjoy the ride even as my mind was arguing. Processing.

Two of them. *At the same time.* The idea didn't scare me as much as it probably should have. But claim a mate together. Mate? As in forever? I knew enough about the other alien warriors, the Prillons and Atlans and the rest of these super-possessive, alpha males to know what that word meant.

"Mate?" I asked. "No. I'm not a mate. I'm no one's mate." Were they crazy? I just wanted a quickie. A good time. A little fun before I had to dive back into the guts and gore and killing fields. *Mate* had barely registered when the second part of what he'd said finally worked its way through my sex-fogged brain. "Wait. Bite? Did you say *bite*?"

Blinking in confusion, I looked back at Blade, who grinned. I thought I'd seen everything during my time in space. This? I never imagined fangs.

Yes. Fangs.

3

tyx

OUR MATE LOOKED DAZED AS BLADE CARESSED HER, KISSED her skin, her neck, but she didn't fight my hold. When she'd walked into the bar, the air had left my lungs as if I'd been punched, and my cock grew instantly hard. Now? I couldn't let her go. I needed her just like this, her arms over her head, her body open and trusting. Exposed. Vulnerable.

She didn't understand it, this immediate connection. I recognized it where I knew females from Earth did not. Especially one who had not come through the Brides Program. I only knew one Earth female. Katie. She'd been beautiful and wild, just like Harper. But she hadn't made me wild in return. Eager, yes, but not for her. She belonged to another, an Everian Hunter who would kill to keep her.

I understood that driving need to both possess and protect now that I held Harper in my arms. Harper belonged to me and Blade. There was no question. No doubt. She was mine, and I'd kill anyone who tried to keep her from me, tried to hurt her.

As if she'd been made for me, she instinctively gave me what I needed. Trust. Passion. Her golden hair was like a beacon, her green eyes so expressive I could see into her soul. I saw everything there. Her desire, her fear. She hid nothing, and the animal part of me had already made its decision.

Mine.

There would be no arguing. No resistance. I didn't want to resist, I wanted her. Her hot, wet pussy welcoming me as I filled her. I wanted to hear her guttural cries of pleasure as we pushed her to her limits, making her come over and over until she lost control. I wanted to hear my name on her lips, not as she'd said it now, but with longing in her voice. Affection. Tenderness. I knew I would never grow tired of her lips, or the flavor of her Earthly whiskey on her tongue. I would have to trade someone for the S-Gen programming to ensure she had the drink available.

I watched her mind whirl and spin, calculating and trying to figure out what we wanted, what we were going to do. She'd come of her own free will into the hallway with me, even if she did not fully understand her desire to be mine. I could see the doubt. She thought us insane—perhaps herself as well—making promises she assumed we had no intention of keeping.

She was wrong.

"You are mine now, Harper." I lifted my knee to the juncture of her thighs as Blade kissed her, one hand on her breast, the other cupping her rounded ass.

Her soft moan made my cock ache as I watched Blade

learn her taste. She kissed him back, all resistance gone. Her slight wrists were so slender and delicate, I held her as I might a baby bird, afraid I'd break her, and every second my mind calculated all possible outcomes.

Blade devoured her, his hunger raging at him, as mine had the moment I'd caught her scent. She shivered, melting for us, submitting to us, and I knew I'd made the right decision when Blade offered something we'd never given another—our bite. Our protection.

Forever.

She was Coalition. Her uniform. The blaster at her side. It was all standard issue for the MedRec teams, the medical technicians and clean-up crews who rushed in after battle to help the warriors who could be saved. I'd been on those killing fields many times myself, not to save lives, but to scavenge weapons. Tech. Things my legion could sell on the black market. We carefully avoided the healing angels like her. We weren't there to fight, nor to save. We were there out of necessity.

By Coalition standards, my people were criminals. Outcasts. Zenith was a hub for both civilian and military activity, owned by the Coalition, but not a military base. This place existed in the gray area between what would have been a utopian world and reality. Cold, hard reality.

My world.

Blade lifted her gently, moving her so her clit rubbed the hard length of my thigh over and over, rolling her hips with the steady press and release of his firm grip on her ass. She gasped, tearing her mouth from his as he continued to cup and play with her breasts with his free hand, first one, then the other.

She was shaking now, her pale skin flushed pink, her

lips swollen and red and ripe. I longed to watch them stretch around my cock as I fucked that sweet mouth, as I claimed every inch of her.

"Wait," she breathed.

Blade and I both froze, looking at our mate, waiting for her to continue.

"Wait. Stop. I—this is crazy."

She was not unaffected. The opposite was true. Perhaps her reaction frightened her, was too strong. "It is not crazy to want what we can give you. Many females on our world have hoped for what we offer you."

"Many females, huh?" She bit her lip and turned her head away from both of us. "I'm no mate, boys. I thought I might have some fun with you." She glanced at me, then at Blade. "But both of you would be pretty damn hot. We might have some fun, but that's it."

"Why?" Strange. She'd been instantly attracted and had ventured into the hallway with me for privacy. Even said she was interested in being with both of us. Now she'd changed her mind? Had we overwhelmed her with talk of forever? I could not lie to her. I intended to keep her, and she needed to accept that fact as quickly as possible. She was mine.

"Why? Because I'm not looking for a mate." Her gaze darted to mine and I saw the confusion in her eyes, the anxious look as she risked a glance at Blade. "Or two."

I frowned, wondering why she tormented herself with such resistance. She'd been on the brink of coming—from just riding my thigh. Why had she stopped? Why deny herself such pleasure? I wanted to watch her come, watch her eyes glaze and lose focus. Know I was the reason she lost control. I wanted her to trust me enough to lose that control, craved that intimacy, that secret, passionate part of her.

"You're scared," I said, studying her closely. I would share her with Blade, but no one else. Blade was closer than any brother, and I would trust no other to help me keep her safe. "Scared to have two lovers?"

"Um, no. I've—never mind. The past doesn't matter."

She flushed a bright crimson, her neck and face turning an intriguing shade of pink. Embarrassed? "You've taken two lovers before?" I asked.

She nodded and my smile nearly hurt. "Good. Then what are you afraid of?"

"We won't hurt you," Blade offered, leaning in close once more, his lips brushing her cheek. "We will take care of you. Protect you. Worship you."

She shook her head, quivering in my grasp.

"Still afraid? Of us?" Blade asked.

Harper shook her head. "No. Not you. Your fangs? That you'll bite me? Uh, yeah." She tugged at my hold on her wrists, and I refused to let her go. Not now, not when she discovered how we would claim her. It would have been so much easier if our mate had come from Rogue 5, but no. We had to find a female who knew nothing about us, about our need to bite our mate as we fucked her in order to claim her. To mark her with our teeth at the juncture of her neck and shoulder. The idea even more daunting with both me and Blade since we would claim her together.

Not all Hyperions would share a mate. There were no laws regarding this. Hell, there weren't many laws at all on Rogue 5. We did what we wished within our own rules, rules that had to be obeyed.

Rules I made.

Rules I now wanted to break. For her.

Blade breathed her in, his eyes drifting closed in

27

pleasure she could not see as he absorbed her into himself. Memorized her scent, as I had. "We will not bite you here. Now. Not in the back hallway of a canteen."

"So, you'll save the vampire act for later. Oh, well, that makes me feel so much better. That solves *everything*."

Sarcasm dripped from every word. And what in the name of the gods was a vampire?

"Do not fear the claiming. By the time we sink our fangs into your flesh, you will be begging for it," Blade whispered into her hair and she shivered, eyes closed, the movement passing through her entire body and into mine. Yes. She wanted us. Needed us. Needed this.

She huffed. "When I finish my time in my MedRec unit, I go back to Earth. You guys are barking up the wrong tree with this mating and biting stuff."

"It is not our teeth that you fear," I said. "It's yourself."

Her eyes flashed open and her gaze locked on mine. Yes, I saw the flash of vulnerability, the surprise that I could find the truth lurking in her brain. She hid it well, deflected her fears onto our fangs to hide her true concern. She may fear the bite, but she feared her attraction to us more.

"Are you afraid to come?" Blade asked.

When she rolled her eyes, I knew he was nowhere close.

"She's afraid to come...for us." She closed her eyes on a soft sigh. Yes, my words were more accurate. "You worry that you're too responsive? That you want us too much? That you won't be able to stop?"

She offered a small laugh. "Fine. We'll skip the whole fang thing for now. How can I be this attracted, this turned on by a male alien I just met in a bar? And his friend? It scares me a little, yes. I don't even know you. So, this is, by definition, completely insane."

"You don't know us...yet."

Her hips shifted. "I know. It's just—"

Blade ran a finger down the outside of her arm. "Intense?"

She nodded her head against the wall. "There are two of you. I, um...thought I might want a quickie, some fun to make me forget for a little while before I get called out again, but this? You guys are...intense."

It was my turn to smile, pleased to hear she felt this... this connection between us just as abruptly and just as deeply. My gaze flicked to Blade's and we didn't need to speak. He felt it, too.

"You need to come," I said, seeing the need, the ache, in every soft curve, in every breath.

She nodded her head.

"We will not fuck you here. I prefer a bed. And privacy."

"And you naked," Blade added. His eyes roved over her as did his hand, learning her.

"That, too," I added. "But you're needy, so let your mates give you the release you need."

"You're not my mates," she countered, squirming again.

I inwardly sighed. She was not from Hyperion or even Rogue 5 on the outer moons. She was from Earth. While Katie had a mark that made her an Everian descendant, it seemed that Harper was a pure Earthling and had no innate understanding of having a mate. Or two. We were not getting anywhere by pushing the mate issue on her now. It was wrong of me to do so, especially when I wanted to see her face when she found her pleasure. We would give her what she needed now and then resolve the "mate" issue later. And the biting. I had no doubt she'd bring that back up, but if she was this responsive just standing in a hallway, by the time we claimed her, she would not be afraid. She'd be completely mindless with need.

"You will come," I said, lowering my voice and issuing it as a command, not as a question. She would do as I said, even in this.

Her eyes, before now, were a little wild and too focused on what we were doing. She was panicking. But after those three words, her gaze met mine, her pupils dilated so most of the deep green disappeared and she focused. On me.

"Look at me," I ordered and her gaze locked to mine. Held.

I lowered her arms and shifted so my back was against the wall, spun her about and pulled her in front of me, positioning her back so it pressed to my chest.

Blade watched with a knowing grin on his face, waiting patiently for what I was about to offer him.

Our mate's sweet, wet pussy.

"What are you—" My mate never finished her question as I tangled my hand in her hair at the base of her neck and angled her chin up until our lips nearly collided. The position left her turned and vulnerable. Open to Blade's attention.

I lowered my lips to brush hers and whispered. "Blade is going to lower your pants and taste you, Harper. He's going to suck your clit into his mouth and make you scream."

Harper panted, her eyes dilated with desire as I tugged on her hair. The slight twinge of pain made her gasp, her heart racing in her chest faster than I'd ever heard, as frantic as she was. "Do you want to come?" I asked.

Blade's hands settled on her hips, at the waist of her pants, and we waited for her response.

A shudder passed through her, but she held my gaze. "Yes."

Lips still barely touching hers, I held her still as Blade undid the fastening on the front of her pants, tugged them down so her pussy was exposed. While I had no direct view, Blade did, and I watched as his jaw clenched with need. He licked his lips as if he were salivating to get a taste. We were both on high alert, listening for unwanted company, but I knew this station, knew most of its people. Unless her nosy team members came looking for her, no one would dare interrupt.

Blade dropped to his knees before our mate, who still stood, legs slightly parted, but not enough. She hadn't given us everything, not yet, was still hanging on to a thread of control.

"Open your legs, Harper," I commanded.

Blade shook his head. "Not enough. I want her spread wide for me."

He yanked at one of her boots, tugged it off, then worked her pants down and off one leg. Hooking a hand behind her bare knee, he placed it over his shoulder so she was open and exposed for him. Perfect.

"Don't move until Blade gives you permission. Do you understand?"

She swallowed, hard, and settled, giving herself over to what we were doing to her. The simple gesture was submission. Trust. It was so sweet. I held her weight so she was wide open, her pussy on display. Open and eager for Blade's mouth.

Leaning back just a bit, I watched her cheeks flush, heard her breathing change.

Blade slid his hands along her thighs to her pussy lips

31

and spread her open, his body tensing with barely controlled lust. He leaned close, his tongue sliding over her folds just once as a shudder racked his body. "She's hot and so fucking wet for us, Styx. Dripping."

He waited for my next command, knew if he touched her before I gave permission, I'd torture him, make them both wait. Harper was mine. Blade was mine. Their pleasure was mine as well. The need to control them both was pure animal instinct, and I didn't fight it, not when I was in a battle, and not when I held a willing female in my thrall. That Harper was my mate only increased my drive to dominate.

Blade held perfectly still, her wet pussy lips held open and ready for his tongue. His fingers. His cock.

But that I would not allow. Not here.

Her pussy was mine, and I would not take it here, in a hallway. When I fucked her, I would take my time, fill her over and over for hours.

Silence thickened in the hallway like a drug, and I watched her expression change, fascinated by the unfiltered honesty I saw in her eyes. Holding her weight on my thighs, I used my free hand to explore the curve of her breast, her hip.

Unable to deny myself, I dipped lower, to her wet heat, and speared deep, buried two fingers in her wet pussy.

Her moan made my cock throb as I worked her just enough to get her to the edge, but not over. Blade's gaze followed the movement of my hand, transfixed. He breathed deeply as her scent filled the hallway. Sweet, musky, addictive.

When she was shaking, her head loose in my hold, I

stopped, removed my fingers, licked them. Gods, she tasted so good.

"Styx." My name on her lips was a sound I would never forget, her cheeks flushed, her body trembling on the edge of release. "Please."

"Blade will taste you now, but you will not come without permission. Do you understand? You will look at me, keep your eyes open. But do not come."

"I can't—"

Blade's mouth locked onto her clit and she bucked in my arms, her words forgotten.

"Fuck her with your fingers, Blade. Feel how tight and hot she is. But don't let her come."

His grin was wild, filled with eagerness, and I knew he would not argue.

I studied her expression, learning every nuance and flicker of emotion as Blade worked her clit with his mouth, her hips rocked forward and back, her lush ass rested on top of my hard thighs.

So perfect. So responsive. So submissive.

Her gaze was locked onto mine, but her eyes were unfocused, unseeing, lost in what Blade was doing to her body.

He started and stopped, teasing her as I'd ordered him to do. She knew, her body pliant and soft in my arms. Blade worked her until the dazed look was replaced by frantic need, until she tugged against the hand I still held buried in her hair hard enough to make her eyes water, one word falling from her lips over and over.

"Please, please, please." The chant was quiet, desperate, not really words but though a constant plea.

"Look at me." My voice was hard, commanding, and her gaze cleared long enough for me to make sure she knew who held her, who controlled her body now, who she belonged to.

"You're mine, Harper. Say it."

"Yes."

With a smile I knew was more animal than man, I lifted my free hand and wrapped it around her neck.

As I suspected, her eyelids fluttered and closed, her entire body responding to the dominance in my touch, melting. Satisfied at last, I leaned down and brushed her ear with my lips.

"Come, Harper. Come now."

The command set her off like an ion blast, and I kissed her to bury the scream as Blade conquered her pussy, fucked her with his fingers, sucked her clit, made her buck and whimper and lose all sense of herself.

He made her come again and again, until she shook in my arms, tears streaming down her cheeks.

I kissed them away as Blade brought her down slowly, gently. His kisses no longer rough or demanding, but gentle. Soft. Full of tenderness, meant to soothe rather than arouse.

"Harper?" I released her hair to cup her cheek in my hand. She was so small, so delicate. The sight of her surrender one I would never grow tired of.

Her chin tipped up, her mouth fell open just as her eyes closed. "Yes," she breathed, her muscles lax as I held her and Blade's hands roamed her legs and hips in slow, gentle motions meant to calm our wild mate.

"You're beautiful," I murmured, unwilling to move from my position along the wall, unable to give her up. The press of my cock against her lower back was almost painful, my

34

balls drawn up tight and ready to flood her with my seed. But not here, in a bed and then I would—

A beeping came from her wrist, and I glanced down, noticed the lighted band about her wrist was no longer a light blue, but red.

"Gods, no. Her wrist unit is signaling," Blade said, his worried gaze lifting to mine, a question there. We knew what the wrist unit was for, what it meant for our mate. Were we really going to allow Harper to go off on another mission? Alone? Unprotected? Especially now that we'd seen her come, knew the level of trust she put in us? The rage building behind his eyes one I recognized. He was not pleased with the idea.

Neither was I.

But Harper was not part of Styx legion. She was human, and a Coalition officer. We weren't here to start a war with the Coalition Fleet. And our little mate might be submissive right now, may have her well-satisfied pussy on display for us, but if we tried to stop her from doing her duty? I had a feeling Harper's sweetness was conditional, her trust temporary. For her, this thing between us—what had she called it—*a quickie*?

Harper was completely still except for her deep breaths, the rise and fall of her lush breasts. I loved seeing her like this, so blissed out with pleasure she didn't even recognize her wrist unit was summoning her.

She didn't process Blade's words until I shook my head at him and lifted my chin toward her clothes in a silent command to put her boot and pants back on.

He lowered her leg from his shoulder. The motion brought her back to herself as I released my grip on her neck and face, lowered my hands carefully to her sides to support her as Blade got her dressed. "Harper," I breathed.

This time, when the beeps came from her wrist unit, they were louder and she came back to herself. I watched her rein in her thoughts, her feelings, watched the transformation from satisfied lover to efficient Coalition crew in the space of a few heartbeats.

Her control made my cock jump, and I fought to keep my fangs from bursting from my mouth. I wanted to bite her. Mark her. Scent her. Claim her. Now. Right fucking now.

But I was not a Hyperion animal; I was a man. I was Styx, a legion of names tattooed into my flesh with the weight of the lives I was responsible for protecting.

I could not bring the entire Coalition down on the legion by kidnapping this female. She was mine. I would not leave Zenith station without her, but I would have to find another way.

"Shit. Latiri 4 again." She pulled away from me and slammed her foot into the boot Blade had begun to work on with an adeptness I knew came from months of training. She was completely focused now, controlled, without fear or panic at the mission ahead of her. Knowing she'd given up that precious control to us just moments ago made something deep in my chest ache. She was fierce now, beautiful and fierce and able to push her pleasure aside for duty with a cold efficiency I couldn't help but admire.

My mate could more than survive the law of the legions. Perhaps she could thrive there. With me.

With us.

Blade removed his hand from her body and stepped

back when she shoved him away. I was next, dismissed with a gentle pat on the shoulder, as if I were a pet.

I tried not to take her dismissal personally, but vowed to make her pay for the lack of respect later.

She would never dismiss me again. Never forget who she belonged to. Once she was mine, there would be no doubt, no walking away.

But now wasn't the time to revel in this knowledge, or to do anything about it. She was being summoned to another post-battle deployment. She had a job to do. And unless I were willing to sacrifice lives by starting a conflict with the Coalition, I had no choice but to let her go.

A fierce wave of protectiveness washed over me, swamping me with a sensation of...panic? While I knew her role on Zenith, the danger she faced hadn't affected me until now, until we'd tasted her, held her, saw her come. Now, I wanted to toss her over my shoulder and return to Rogue 5 where she would be safe. Not only from my enemies, but from her own job.

But no. We had no claim on her. Yet. If I took her now, not only would she resist, but I'd be breaking about a dozen laws of the Interstellar Coalition Fleet. They left me alone because I steered clear of their notice.

Kidnapping a member of one of the MedRec units, and a female member at that, would earn me the attention of thousands of warriors intent on saving her.

The Prillons, the Atlans, the Trions and even the humans, were protective of their women. If I tried to take her against her will, I'd have a small army of ships barreling down on Rogue 5 within days.

No. She had to come willingly. Now was not the time. She was our mate *because* of who she was, of what she was.

A healer. Fearless. Brave. We had to let her go. It would kill me to do so, but the beeping wrist unit wasn't just a notice for her to deploy, but for us to accept her departure.

She gasped, stiffened when she returned fully to herself. "Shit. I'm so sorry," she mumbled, lifting her wrist. "I...I have to go."

Blade stood to his full height. He stepped back, allowed her passage.

She glanced at me, then Blade. "This has been...fun. Thanks for—you know."

Blade nodded, remaining silent. His hands were clenched at his sides, as if he was holding himself back from grabbing her, from keeping her from going. He felt the loss as keenly as I, and she was still with us.

I couldn't speak now, couldn't tell her we would be awaiting her return, that when she came back healthy and whole, we would continue where we left off, that it would be my turn to be on my knees for her, to taste her—and not just licking her flavor from my fingers. There was no time. She was needed immediately.

She offered a quick nod, then dashed down the hall in a quick sprint.

She may have gotten away this time, but we could use the time she was working to learn more about her role, how much longer she was required to serve the fleet. And how to get her out of that particular duty without starting a war I couldn't win. I glanced at Blade, knew his thoughts.

He shifted his cock in his pants. If he was as hard as me, nothing was going to ease the discomfort except our mate's eager pussy.

"If she's officially mated, she can no longer go into combat zones."

"We are not part of the Coalition Fleet. We can't claim a mate."

"Bullshit," Blade argued. "That bastard at the Intelligence Core offered us a lot of perks we've never taken advantage of. Including being processed for an Interstellar Bride."

Blade was right, but I didn't want to call the Prillon bastard, Doctor Mersan. He was a spy, his heart as black and merciless as the cold of deep space. "What if we submit to that process and we aren't matched to her?"

Running his hands through his long silver hair, Blade snarled. "You're right. She won't be in the The Colony database anyway. She's in MedRec. We'd be matched to someone else. Fuck."

"Exactly. And I don't want Doctor Mersan to know about her. She'll give him too much leverage over us."

Blade slammed his palm flat against the wall in frustration. "How much longer? How long does the Coalition own her?"

"I don't know." But I intended to find out. And the moment we could take her without endangering the rest of the legion, she'd be safe on Rogue 5, and in my bed.

arper, Battlefield Medical Recovery Mission, Sector 437, Latiri Star Cluster

GRAVEL AND DUST CRUMBLED BENEATH MY FEET AS I RAN FROM body to body, the team moving around me like a swarm of ants. We'd done this so many times we didn't need to talk to know where each of us would go. We had a pattern, a rhythm that worked for us, that got the job done, especially here. This planet, this sector of space was hell. Literally. Hell. Constant battles with the Hive. So much fighting. I could walk this rock without a map.

We naturally split into three teams of five with two fight-ready Prillon warriors on protection duty, guarding the transport pad—and us—as we scurried around the field hunting for survivors.

I was triage, looking for signs of life. Rovo carried the portable transporter devices—a transport patch. They were small but powerful, the size of a silver dollar. When we found someone who needed immediate transport, Rovo would attach the device with a quick slap of his palm against the patient, hit a button and *voila*. Gone. Directly back to Zenith for immediate medical attention.

Somehow, the device moved the person to the nearest full-sized transport, like a game of leapfrog. Yeah, it was space aged and too advanced and techy for me to understand. The first time I saw it work, I was impressed. Now? I wasn't impressed by much of anything at all.

Okay, I was impressed by the way Styx and Blade had made me come. No, I was impressed by the way they got me so hot for them that I let Blade drop to his knees, toss my leg over his shoulder and eat me out as if he were starving. In a hallway! But the end of my orgasm drought wasn't for me to think about now. I'd tuck that steamy memory away for when I got back to Zenith and was alone in my tiny quarters.

For now, I had to think about the massive Atlan warrior on the ground before me. He was huge. Heavy. Just like the rest of these aliens. Pack on their gear, and some of them probably weighed three-fifty. I worked out. I was strong. But not that strong. Not when this small area of battlefield was littered with well over a hundred wounded and scores more dead. And the fact that we were over a hundred feet from the pad.

I lifted my arm to signal Rovo for a transport patch. "Got one."

He finished placing a patch for one of my teammates and walked on to another who signaled him. I'd have to wait because there were too many in need. He'd get here in a minute. Until then, my job was to keep this warrior alive.

The Atlan blinked up at me, his eyes glazed. Unfocused.

I pressed a bandage to a gaping wound in his shoulder and he growled. God, he was huge.

Just what I needed. A full-on berserker moment with a beast. "Don't you dare go beast on me, Atlan, or I'll leave you out here to rot."

The Atlan chuckled, some of his beast receding before my eyes, and the tension in my jaw and shoulders lessened enough that I could move again. Sometimes they were so out of it, they couldn't focus. Sometimes, we couldn't save them.

"You are a bossy female." His voice was as rough and gravely as the ground he laid on.

I smiled down into his face. "Of course. I'm human."

He grinned, then groaned as I tightened the bandage on his arm and ran the ReGen wand over it to help stanch the bleeding. It would help, but not enough to heal. This guy needed a dip in the blue coffins, the ReGen pods back at Zenith.

"I know. My friend Nyko is mated to one of you bossy Earth females."

"Then he's a lucky man." I laughed at the huge, wolfish grin the Atlan gave me. He was tough, I'd give him that. Lying here, bleeding everywhere, *dying*. Cracking jokes. "You need a ReGen Pod, Atlan. Then you'll be all better and can get a bossy Earth female of your own."

"Wulf. My name is Wulf. And I want nothing to do with human females."

"Yeah? Sounds bitter to me."

He grunted as I ran the ReGen wand over the rest of him, but it wasn't enough. He'd been shredded. The front of his armor was in tatters, as if he'd been in a fight with a grizzly bear back home, one with six-inch claws. "What the hell happened to you, Wulf? These cuts aren't from a blaster." He really needed to get out of here. Where was that damn transport beacon? I glanced up looking for Rovo, but he was nowhere to be seen.

Rovo was the second-in-command, and I'd been assigned to his team the moment I'd arrived from Earth. He was a hard-ass, smack-talking former Army medic from L.A. Having the same hometown put us on the same side during debates on most topics, from football to good Mexican food. Rovo was his family name, Italian. I didn't know his first name and didn't ask. Not out here. Names didn't really matter out here. You were either Hive, or you fought them. There was no middle ground. No negotiating.

"Your friend disappeared behind that rock." Wulf struggled to lift his hand and point to where a few black and gray boulders dotted the landscape. It wasn't far away, maybe the length of a football field, but...

Wulf coughed and there was blood on his lips.

Damn. Damn. Damn. I couldn't leave him.

What the fuck was Rovo doing?

Turning the ReGen wand to a locked "on" position, I wedged the base between one of the large openings in Wulf's armor where he'd been slashed open. I shoved it in as Wulf grunted in pain.

"Sorry." *Not sorry.* "It'll keep you alive."

"Sadist."

"You know it." I grinned at Wulf even as I thought about killing Rovo when I saw him next. Kill. Him. Slowly. But even as I thought it, I worried. This wasn't like him. Had he seen more wounded beyond that rock? Did he need help?

Shit. Something was wrong. I could feel it. Glancing around, you'd think nothing was amiss. The others were doing their jobs. Everyone working quietly and efficiently to get this done, get the wounded tagged and shipped out so we could go back to Zenith and recover. Get off this rock. This wasteland.

With the ReGen wand working in futility to heal Wulf's massive chest, I made to stand. "I'll come back for you."

"No." The Atlan's command was sharp. Biting. Good. Maybe the wand was helping more than I thought.

I glanced from Wulf's determined face to the rocks. Something. Was. Not. Right.

But I couldn't let Wulf lie here and die either. He wouldn't last long.

I scanned the others in MedRec, looking for their transport member.

They were all too far away, scattered on the battle area. Damn. I looked from Wulf to the transport pad, judged the distance. We were close. It was his best chance.

And I was going to kill Rovo when I saw him.

"Come on, soldier. On your feet." I wedged my arm beneath his uninjured shoulder and tugged, hard. Nothing. He didn't even budge.

God, he was heavy.

The teasing light in Wulf's eyes faded as his gaze darted from the rocks back to my face.

I looked down and met his dark eyes. "Walk or die, Wulf. Because your free ride out of here is in trouble on the other side of those rocks, and I can't carry you."

Tugging again, I braced my legs under me and got him into a sitting position.

"Move it, Wulf! Move it now!" I yelled at him, I knew, but sometimes these guys didn't listen to anything else. I knew he was hurting and tired and flirting with death. Maybe his beast would respond to a little aggressiveness.

And I was banking on the fact that he was tough as nails and wasn't willing to let go of life just yet.

Wulf struggled to his feet, and I braced myself under his shoulder. "Come on. One step at a time."

"Bossy." He hissed through gritted teeth, but we moved. One step. Two. Three. My back felt like it was going to crack under his weight, but we inched forward. "What's your name?"

"Harper."

"That is not a proper name."

"That's what my dad always said, too." I grinned, watching the ground as we moved, careful for anything that might make us stumble. I'd gotten him to stand once, but I doubted I'd be able to do it again. "But my mom won that argument."

"Bossy, too." He wheezed.

"Yes. Stop talking and walk faster." It only took a couple of minutes, but it felt like an hour as we neared the transport pad and one of the Prillon warriors came down to help. He couldn't leave the pad, I knew that, but I was relieved when we were close enough for him to bend the rules. "Get him to a ReGen pod, now!" I yelled.

The Prillon nodded and took Wulf from me as the giant Atlan slumped onto the pad. He was watching me as I backed away. "You'll be all right, Wulf. Get him to that pod," I ordered again. I glanced over my shoulder picking up the pace, my internal alarm bells going crazy now. Where the hell was Rovo? "Get him out of here!"

Running, I sprinted toward the boulders where Wulf said Rovo had gone when a rumble sounded, the growling thunder of some kind of shuttle engine, and it was coming from the wrong direction.

Oh, God. "Get them all out of here! Now!" I yelled the order. I wasn't second-in-command, but with Rovo missing, I gave the orders on this side of the field.

I didn't know what I expected, but it wasn't the two small shuttles that landed on the edge of the battlefield. And it wasn't the dozen or so mercenaries who stepped out of them. Their armor was black. Half men, half women, they all had a fierceness to their faces I recognized. Some had silver hair, like Blade. Some were dark, like Styx. But they all had the distinct features of the two men I'd almost fucked in that hallway. That time with them up close and personal made it easy for me to know where these mercenaries were from. Rogue 5.

Their uniforms were nearly identical to what Styx and Blade wore, right down to the arm bands around their biceps.

Except the bands weren't silver. They were red. Dark red, like wine. Like dried blood. One of them looked up, saw me watching him. I met his pale gaze and saw nothing there. No heat in his eyes, not like Styx or Blade. No interest or emotion. Only indifference. Even though I was sweating, a chill raced down my spine. His glance alone showed me what I needed to know.

These mercenaries were cold-blooded killers.

Screaming at everyone to get the hell out of there, I ran for Rovo's location, toward the place Wulf said he'd gone. I had to warn him. Find him.

Chaos erupted on the ground as the Prillon on the transport pad opened fire at the new and surprising enemy. They weren't Hive and that scared the crap out of me.

My team fired as well, and the quiet ground covered with the dead and dying exploded in bedlam and screaming.

"Rovo!" I yelled as I pulled my own blaster. I was too far away to fire into the fray, but I had no idea what I'd find when I rounded that huge boulder.

I didn't make it. Three warriors almost as big as Styx appeared around the supersized rock and walked toward me.

Shit. Shit. Shit.

They were too close. I was quick in a lot of ways, but running wasn't one of them. Right now, I wished I had the speed of an Everian Hunter.

Turning on my heel, I ran with every ounce of strength in me. A blast whizzed past my head, and I ducked, weaving and hoping I could dodge the enemy fire. I heard one of my pursuers go down in a tangle of cursing and screaming.

Looking ahead, I saw Wulf on his knees, ion rifle in hand, taking aim behind me again. He was more beast than Atlan, but that was keeping us both alive. The Prillon were firing into the melee on the other side of the field, where the rest of my team was engaged in a battle they appeared to be losing.

Heavy breathing. The loud strike of boots behind me.

Wulf fired again and another of my attackers went down.

"Down!" he bellowed, and I hit the ground rolling as huge hands tangled for purchase in the back of my green uniform before falling away. I took off running again. Wulf fired, I dropped to the ground, but his shot missed as the mercenary chasing me dove for cover.

Scrambling onto my hands and knees, I made it the rest of the way to the transport pad. There, I found Wulf slumped over, unconscious. One of the Prillon warriors looked at me. "Get on. Now! We've got orders to clear the pad so Commander Karter can get his warriors down here."

Warriors? Karter? What?

Impatient, the Prillon grabbed me and lifted me onto the pad. He stepped off, firing into the battle, doing what he could to protect the rest of my team.

"Do it!" he ordered his companion who stood at the controls on the opposite side of the transport. They weren't leaving, I realized. They were going to stay here and fight.

I glanced at Wulf and saw his blood pooling, the ReGen wand on the pad a couple feet away where it had fallen. Damn it.

Crawling toward him, I turned the wand back on and placed it lying on his chest before picking up his ion rifle.

The pad buzzed with energy that made my hair and skin crackle as the power built. I raised the rifle and took aim, taking down one of the mercenaries who'd been firing on my team from a safe distance.

Bastard. Coward.

I had a list of names for men like these.

Behind him, his friends were dragging the wounded and my team away, alive, onto the shuttles.

Why? What the hell?

They were taking weapons, too. Anything and everything they could. But why the warriors? Why my team? Why...

I fired again. The shot hit, but didn't take him down. He turned in my direction, his fangs extended in a feral hiss as he narrowed his eyes at me in rage.

"Shit. Me. I'm. Oh fuck," I gasped after hitting the comm unit on my wrist.

Fangs. I remembered seeing them on Styx when he grinned. Blade, too. But they hadn't been dangerous. No, I hadn't felt fear or panic as I did now looking at one of their own. I'd felt exhilarated. Scared. So hot I couldn't stop thinking about the bite they'd promised me. I had closed my eyes and wanted their mouths on me. Wanted the pain. Wanted to belong to them, be between them. Forget the world and let them have their wicked way with me.

Were these Styx's people? Was this, somehow, his doing? Could he have been fake? Was his '*business associate*' one of these assholes? Was he being all alpha and dominant to me, yet ruthless and murderous with others? He said he was the leader. Was his interest in me, in my team, just a set-up so he could do *this*? Did he mean for me to die along with the others? If warriors didn't get here soon from the battleship, we would all die.

Because of Styx? And Blade.

Furious at the thoughts whirling in my mind, I aimed again. Fired. Watched with satisfaction as the fanged asshole fell over. I wasn't a killer, but rage sparked in me, wrath like I'd never known as I watched the monsters swarm my team. We were no warriors. We were doctors. Nurses. We saved lives, and they were attacking us like we were the enemy.

The energy field built to a near crescendo, and I knew transport was imminent as I took aim at another of the red-armed mercenaries. My finger tightened on the trigger, but he was too fast, to agile. He avoided the ion burst and came closer. He shot one of the Prillon warriors who doubled over in pain but didn't go down.

"Transport initiated!" the other Prillon yelled at me, and

it was the only warning I got before the pain hit. Warping. Twisting agony. Transport technology officially sucked.

From the ground next to the transport pad, the mercenary who'd been chasing me before sprang up and landed on my legs as I pulled the trigger once with a scream. He had hold of me and wasn't going to let go.

He pulled, trying to drag me with him off the pad but Wulf's huge hand tangled in the back of my uniform and held on tight.

The fabric of my uniform cut into my flesh as the two massive men pulled me between them. I raised my rifle right at the mercenary's face, his nose inches from the end of my weapon. I looked down, into his eyes, knew I had to fire again.

Hesitated as nausea roiled in my belly.

I didn't want to do this. When I shot across the field to save my friends? I'd acted on instinct. But this was me. And him. Up close and personal.

His eyes were brown. Full of intelligence and resignation.

Bracing myself, I squeezed the trigger.

Too late.

Everything disappeared and we were pulled into the nothing in-between of transport.

lade, Transport Station Zenith, Transport Docks

THE DOOR TO THE TRANSPORT AREA SLID OPEN, AND IT WAS fucking chaos. The battle station beacon had been blaring for five minutes, the lights in the entire complex turned a muted red. Fully armored warriors rushed by to join teams gathering for transport to the surface, only to be waylaid by orders from Commander Karter himself.

He was sending in a full contingent from the battleship, and Zenith was to stand down and do its job, acting as a relay station for the long-distance transport of the battle group to the Latiri system.

Which meant clearing the transport pads. Nothing in. Nothing out. Not until the troops made it to the ground.

I eased closer to one of the communication crew. He shouted to the officer on deck, who relayed orders to the transport team. It was all very efficient, as if they'd done this a hundred times.

But they'd never been stranding my mate on a foreign planet before. Never endangered her life with their delays.

Styx and I had been in our quarters when the alarm came down, and we'd overheard in the hallway that while Zenith itself was safe, the MedRec team on the ground was being attacked. I'd looked to Styx and we hadn't had to say a word.

Harper.

She was part of the group of healers deployed to the latest post-battle mess in the Latiri system. She'd left us, mindless and satisfied as I'd used my mouth and fingers to get her off. Several times. Yeah, she was that quick to arouse. That sensitive to us. And yet she'd left, gone off to do her job. To save lives, not be caught in the thick of a fucking battle. And I still had the taste of her on my tongue, the scent of her clinging to my fingers.

Our mate was in danger, and there was nothing we could do about it here. It was difficult to work our way to the communication station. First the hallways had been crowded with all the Coalition fighters suiting up for battle and on-site defensive teams staging for potential enemy attack. We'd finally made it to the transport docks only to be shoved aside as transport pads were cleared of supplies and orders given to other stations and planets to delay transport. Everyone had a job to do. Everyone but us.

While we didn't have a role to fulfill—we were here meeting Styx's Coalition contact to acquire weapons and explosives for sale—we had a mate to protect, to save. And the only place to do that was to transport to wherever the fuck Harper was.

We were fully armed, our armor completely charged and ready to absorb ion blasts. I grabbed the communication officer's shoulder. "Where is the MedRec team?"

"Latiri 4. Fifth battle this week," he answered without turning to see who asked the question.

My heart felt as if it stopped beating. "Hive? They're being attacked by Hive?"

"No, no, no." He lifted his hand to the comm device covering one ear and ordered another transport station to hold all incoming transports until further notice. Then spared a quick flick of his eyes in my direction. "No. They're under attack. Unknown enemy. Sounds like scavengers."

Styx stiffened beside me, and we made eye contact in silent communication once again. Scavengers? The only fuckers crazy enough to go into the Latiri system would be ours. And since this wasn't a Styx mission, that meant our mate was probably being attacked by a group of mercenaries from one of the other legions on Rogue 5. Killers. Stone cold killers. Slave traders. Gods damn us all.

"We will transport there immediately," Styx ordered, but I was already walking toward the transport pad. We would reach our mate, and everyone else could go to hell. Styx was walking beside me, giving me the space I needed. While he might be the leader of the legion, I was the fighter. He was calm, calculating. He never lost control. I, on the other hand, had a legendary temper. Blade, the rebel. Nothing got in my way, especially when I was fucking pissed.

Someone was putting my mate's life in danger, and I didn't even try to hold myself in check. Styx often joked he thought I wasn't pure Hyperion at all, that my mother had lied about my lineage, and she'd had a wild romp with an Atlan.

I felt like I had an inner beast, wild and ruthless, ready to rip off heads to keep Harper safe. My fangs elongated, my cock hardened. My entire body was primed with adrenaline, ready to wreak havoc. And Styx was giving me room to do so.

As we neared the transport controls, the battle beacon muted, but the red lights persisted. The doors to transport pad 4 opened on our approach to reveal a group of five Coalition fighters, fully decked out in battle armor, preparing to be sent to the site.

I climbed onto the transport pad behind them, Styx falling in next to me.

The Prillon warrior on the controls looked up. "Get off the pad. You're not authorized."

Styx's gaze fixed on the warrior. "My fucking mate is down there. Send us now."

Several of the warriors turned to look at us, took our measure, and must have come to the same conclusion because their leader turned to the control panel. "Do it."

The Prillon shrugged. "I can't, sir."

"Explain," the huge Prillon captain demanded. There were four technicians monitoring the controls. Several voices were coming from the speakers around the room, overlapping each other, making it impossible to understand what was happening. Some static only added to my frustration. Nothing was going right, but none of these people had a mate out there in danger.

The technician was moving his hands, his gaze frantic as he scanned the control. "We've got incoming. I can't override."

"Where's it coming from?"

"The attack zone, sir. Officer on the ground entered an override code."

"Fuck. Clear the pad!" The Prillon captain pulled his helmet off his head and stomped to the controls to see for himself. He was bronze, skin and hair, with fierce yellow eyes. And he was pissed.

"Contact him," the Prillon ordered. "Now!"

The technician did so as we cleared the pad. The sounds of screaming, ion blasters and distant shouting filled the room. Chaos. Battle. I'd heard it enough times.

"Shit. Me. I'm. Oh, fuck." A very feminine voice blasted through the speakers, filled with panic, and my entire being stilled.

Harper's voice. Styx straightened, his hands clenched into fists the only sign of his inner turmoil. In Styx, that was tantamount to a full on meltdown.

I could hear her breathing hard, the garbled words. I knew that sound, felt it deep in my bones. Harper was in trouble. A vise gripped around my heart, squeezed.

"Lieutenant Barrett? Report," the technician replied, no doubt tracking her identity through her Coalition identifier or NPU. When nothing further came from the surface, the Prillon captain took over, his voice booming.

"Zenith to MedRec Unit 4. This is Captain Vanzar. Report."

Her scream pierced the air and everyone stilled.

"Harper!" I shouted, stepping toward the pad. The fighter group raised their weapons on instinct at my sudden outburst and movement. I felt the sizzle, the thrumming of an incoming transport and a hand on my arm held me back. Styx.

A second later, Harper shimmered and appeared, sprawled across the pad. She wasn't alone. An Atlan warrior was a few feet away, bloodied and unconscious. But I didn't give a damn about him. It was the male who had a firm grip on Harper's legs I focused on. They were sprawled on the pad as if he'd leaped through the air and grabbed for her, getting his hold on her lower leg, tripping her just before they transported.

He dug his fingers into her thigh, blood dripping as he snarled at her, using the hold in her flesh to pull her closer. She screamed again, fear written on her face as she pointed an ion rifle squarely in his face. His eyes narrowed and he pulled on her again. She threw her head back in a silent scream, trying to kick him off.

Why didn't she fire?

I saw red. Anger coursed through me, hot and visceral. Harper continued to struggle, to tug at the hold on her leg, her bloody hands trying to find purchase on the smooth metal of the transport pad. Her attacker had the strength to pull her backward, and he reached for her neck, his claws out, a snarl on his face.

He was a dead man. He knew it. He ignored the group of warriors around him, focused on my mate. On her soft, exposed throat as he pulled her closer. His gaze focused on her pulse like a hungry predator

I knew that look, the evil intent behind his hold. I saw myself in him. He wasn't just the enemy, he was also Hyperion. And from Rogue 5. His uniform was identical to mine and Styx's, unrelenting black except for the thin band of red on his arm. The dark red of Cerberus legion.

Except—I knew that face.

"Let me go!" Harper screamed, eyes wild and full of

fear. Her hair had fallen from the tie that had held it out of her face less than an hour earlier when she'd left us in the hallway. Her cheeks were marred with dirt and a smear of blood. Her green uniform was torn at one shoulder and at her right knee. And she was covered in blood.

I leapt up onto the raised dais and ignored Harper. Tending to the attacker meant tending to her. He looked so much like me, silver hair, pale and determined eyes.

At my approach, he redoubled his efforts, scrambling to get the job done. That's what Harper was to him, a kill. An order. As he hooked one hand around Harper's hip and tugged, she fell onto her back with a scream and kicked at him. He was too focused, his intention too finite for the attack on Harper to be random. Perhaps he'd been on the battlefield to eliminate her. At all costs.

With a growl, I launched myself at him. With his hands occupied with my mate, he had no defense.

"I want him alive!" Captain Vanzar roared. Too late. One swift twist of his head—one of my hands settled at the back of his neck, the other wrapped around his jaw—I snapped his spine with a sickening crunch before the bellowed order registered. I tossed his corpse away like trash. Forgotten.

The captain cursed as the body landed on the pad with a thud.

"Damn it all. Arrest him," Captain Vanzar ordered, and six ion blasters turned on me. I ignored them, focused only on Harper now.

"She is my mate," I growled, and all six lowered their weapons.

"Fuck." The Prillon knew I was within my rights to kill the assassin for daring harm her. Every warrior in the room would have done the same. "Check her," he ordered one of the others.

I growled a protest as an Atlan neared her and bent close to her head. When he rose to his full height, he looked at his captain and nodded. "She carries his scent."

"Fine. Take care of your mate, and get the fuck out of my way." He stormed to the transport pad, yelling for a medical team.

Styx tried to grab Harper, but she crawled to the fallen Atlan, shoving Styx's hands away. "Warlord Wulf needs a ReGen Pod, now. Right now!" She screamed the order at two Prillon warriors standing near the edge of the platform, and they jolted into motion, lifting the huge male between them and hurrying toward an approaching team of medical personnel wearing green.

Once her patient was taken care of, she turned to Styx for comfort, and I saw my friend, my leader, shudder in relief as he pulled her into his arms. He carried her down the steps and away from any chance of being transported back to the battle accidently.

"Get us down there. Now!" Captain Vanzar gave the order and his entire unit scrambled onto the transport pad as Styx and I carried Harper farther away.

Seconds later, they were gone. Harper watched them go, a shudder passing through her. "They're too late," she whispered.

I stood to my full height, clenched my hands into fists, tried to control my breathing. It had been too easy, the Hyperion's death. I needed to kill him again. And again. Slowly.

"What happened?" Styx asked. His hands roamed her, searching for injuries. "Are you hurt?"

Impatient, she shoved his hands away. "No. The blood's not mine. It's Wulf's." She craned her neck, perhaps looking for him, perhaps simply watching and listening to the transport team and organized chaos of the transport dock.

"What happened, Harper?" I asked, unable to wait. Afraid to touch her, afraid I'd yank her from Styx's arms. Frighten her further.

"There were three of them. Wulf saved me," Harper said, pushing against Styx's firm hold. He loosened his arms, but didn't release her.

"Three attackers caused all this chaos?" I demanded.

She shook her head, staring at the now empty platform. "No. There were dozens of them. All wearing those arm bands. They were taking everyone. Taking blasters and all of our gear. Loading the survivors onto their shuttles." She blinked, now clinging to Styx. It seemed she couldn't decide if she wanted to push him away or hold him close. "Why would they do that?"

Dozens? Were they planning to attack Zenith as well? Would more of Cerberus' legion come after our mate? "Shut down transports," I said to the technician.

"I don't take orders from you, merc. I've got a battleship unit ready to transport from the Karter. Injured warriors to be brought here to the med unit. The rest of the MedRec group to evacuate. Get your mate out of here. I'm busy."

"Someone tried to kill her—" I bit out the words through clenched teeth. I didn't break his neck solely because Harper was standing in front of me, safe in Styx's arms. "This station isn't safe." I angled my head to the now vacant transport pad.

"Blade." Styx's voice cut through the haze, and I released the transport technician from my gaze, irritated when his shoulders slumped in relief. I turned to my friend, worried for Harper. "He was from Cerberus."

I took a deep breath, let it out. I *knew* that face. Had seen it on Rogue 5 before. "And?"

"Harper isn't safe here. The Coalition can't protect her. Not from Cerberus."

"Cerberus?" she asked, but I didn't clarify. Now wasn't the time. This wasn't the place.

I narrowed my eyes, glanced at Harper who now clung to Styx as if her life depended on it. She was in shock, although she was exceptional at trying to calm her nerves. The panic had lessened in her eyes and some color had returned to her cheeks.

"Tell me something I don't know," I gritted out, responding to Styx's statement.

"We must get her out of here," he added. "Away from this station. We need to take her home. We need her deep inside Styx territory where no one can reach her."

I sighed, let some of the tension leave my body. Styx and I were in complete agreement on this one. "Fuck, yes."

Zenith was under Coalition control. We had no guards here, no one from our legion to offer protection. No one here was loyal to Styx. Here, Coalition rules applied, like keeping the transport pad open to any fucker willing to kill my mate. But within Styx? We ruled. No, we *made* the rules. We could take care of Harper and this new Cerberus problem. I glanced at the dead Hyperion. The uniform.

Why was Cerberus here? Scavenging weapons, yes. But taking survivors? And attacking a Coalition MedRec team? That didn't sound like Cerberus. Their leader kept them focused on covert assignments, high-level assassinations. Thievery. They didn't traffic slaves, and they did not attack

Coalition forces. Moreover, how had they known the MedRec team would be on that planet?

Nothing added up. And why attack Harper? Why follow her here? What had she seen? What the fuck had happened down there?

We weren't going to stay around and find out. More fighters stepped up onto the pad and transported out. They were instantly gone. The injured would come this way next. We weren't needed. Harper had done her job and almost died for it. She wasn't going back out there. No fucking way. Someone would have to snap my neck for that to happen and then get through Styx. And I knew enough about protocol here on Zenith to know what she would face next. I definitely wasn't letting Harper get pulled into hours of questioning with Coalition investigators only to be sent out into the field again. Worse, if we left her here, she'd be vulnerable to any traitor or killer who could make his way onto the station.

Fuck their rules. She'd served them long enough. She belonged to us now.

"We need to get her out of here," Styx repeated. "Now."

"What? Where are you taking me?" Harper asked.

"To Rogue 5, where you'll be safe," I told her.

Her cheek was pressed against Styx's chest, but she glanced up at me. Frowned.

"Why? It's not even Coalition. How can I be safer there?" she asked.

"You'll be protected by us," Styx vowed. "And you'll be safe because there *isn't* any Coalition."

"But he...he's dressed just like you." She reached her arm out, pointed to the dead Cerberus who'd been tugged off the transport pad and now lay sprawled in the corner awaiting some kind of investigation. "He was from Rogue 5, right?"

I nodded and she closed her eyes, her fingers gripping Styx's biceps even harder. "Then we can't go there."

I reached out, pulled Harper out of Styx's hold. Hugged her. Felt her fully against me for the first time. Gods, she felt good. Soft, gentle, small.

"Mine," I growled.

"We will take you to our home where you belong," Styx added.

"Between us," I added.

"It won't be any safer, not if the people who attacked are from your home," she insisted.

"Mate, we are the *only* ones who can keep you safe." Styx approached the lead technician. "The next free transport window, you will send us to Rogue 5, Styx legion."

"There is an open window now," he replied, but did not look up from the controls.

"You didn't see us leave." Styx waited for the Coalition warrior to look up from his controls. "She's my mate and she's being hunted."

The Prillon looked from Styx to me, and finally to Harper, who clung to me, her hands shaking despite the brave face she was putting on. "She's your mate? And he's your second?"

When Prillons mated, there was a primary male and a chosen second to claim their female together. Styx and I were equals. Neither would be a second, even if everyone else would think me one. We would claim her evenly. We'd fuck her together and often apart.

Styx narrowed his eyes. "Yes. And we'll kill anyone who tries to stop us from taking her."

The Prillon almost grinned, just the far corner of his mouth twitching up, clearly understanding that a mate came first. "May the gods witness and protect you." He spoke the formal Prillon ritual words and lifted his chin in the direction of the transport pad. "I never saw you. I'll erase the transport record, but you need to go now. Right now."

"What is your name?"

The Prillon started. "Mykel."

"I am Styx, of the Styx legion on Rogue 5. If you have need, call for me. For helping save my mate, I owe you a life debt."

The Prillon ignored his words, quickly working the controls as I led Harper back up to the transport pad.

"Are you sure about this? They were from your planet," she said, her voice cloaked with exhaustion.

I lifted my hand to her head and held her to my chest, gently stroking the silken strands of her golden hair, soothing her. "Trust us, Harper. We will take care of you."

She had reason to worry. Until we knew why Cerberus was attacking Coalition fighters—and MedRec teams—we would be vulnerable. Cerberus the legion, but also Cerberus the leader. He knew what was going on, what his people were doing. He knew everything.

But we'd be on our turf. Our rules. Our battleground. Thousands of lethal warriors willing to kill to protect Styx, and our new mate. With Harper between us, nothing else mattered. Just her safety and happiness.

I clenched my jaw, hugged Harper tighter to me, feeling the strongest bout of possession.

"By the time I'm done, Cerberus will beg me to end him," Styx said with dark intention, jumping up onto the platform to join us right before the transport began.

tyx, Rogue 5, Styx Legion Core Command Room

"Cerberus doesn't deal in slaves. The female must be mistaken."

"We can't trust her, she's Coalition."

"What is Cerberus doing in that Sector? Is he trying to bring the entire fucking Fleet to our door?"

Raised voices filled the meeting room, jumbled and arguing, one on top of the other in a cacophony of noise.

Still, it felt good to be home, to have my mate tended to. To know she was safe.

I let them argue, waiting for the inevitable verbal battle still to come. I'd told them about Harper, about the attack in Sector 437, the Cerberus uniforms. All of it.

I had yet to reveal to the men and women in this meeting room that Harper, a female from Earth, an active duty Coalition officer, a woman I'd taken from Zenith without permission or following protocol, was my mate.

Standing at the head of the table, I gripped the back of my chair and let the chaos roll through me. I was impervious to the din, knowing Blade had our mate somewhere safe, bathing her, tending her, feeding her. Caring for her as was right and proper. As leader of the legion, I could not always care for a mate as I should, which was why Blade would claim her, too.

When I failed her, called away by duty or necessity like now, Blade would not. Were he out fighting, I would tend to her. This moment I knew I'd made the correct decision, for as disorder swirled around me, knowing my mate was safe and secure with Blade, I was content.

The large stone table before us had been transported from the Hyperion surface to our moon base, the cold connection to our home world a reminder that grounded us in our past, our duty to the ancestors, to protecting not just this moon base, but the sacred beasts on the surface below. The table normally held six seated around its broken edges, myself plus five lieutenants. Soon, with a mate, that number would increase to seven.

If I thought my legion was agitated now—

"Styx saw the uniform as well. Cerberus legion raided Latiri 4. We need to know why." Silver sat opposite my position at the end of the table, Blade's seat next to her noticeably vacant. Khon sat on her right, silently taking in the argument with intelligent pale green eyes and his arms crossed over a massive chest. His face might as well have been a stone wall. He shaved his head, claimed the dark hair interfered with his ability to sense the wind when he was on the surface. Of all of us, he went to the Hyperion surface the most, to hunt. To check on the well-being of our ancestral families, the wild ones still living below. He was brutal and efficient, and slow to anger. Which was why he occupied one of the chairs. "Do we not have spies in Cerberus?"

"Cerberus killed both of our spies last month." Silver's long hair was pulled back tight in a braid, the pale color nearly identical to Blade's, their features similar enough to make their shared mother obvious. But that was where the likeness ended. Blade was quick to fight, quick to anger, and quick to forgive.

Silver was a woman, a Hyperion female. She rarely raised her voice, and like Khon next to her, was a cold, calculating strategist. But lose her trust and she'd kill you as soon as look at you. There was no forgiveness in her. Her gaze met mine, and what I saw there made me ball my hand into a fist at my side in silent warning. She was tall, like all Hyperion females, and strong. But it was her mind the others feared. And her ruthlessness. Like all females from our world, she was merciless when it came to protecting her family. And this legion was her family now. Her brother, Blade, my second-in-command, and now my mate-bonded, was the only blooded family she had left.

She was listening. For now. But I knew, should I fail to maintain my dominance in this room, any one of the four at the table could rise in challenge to take leadership of the Styx legion from me. And the only way to win was a fight to the death. *My death.*

Silver would be first.

Khon and Silver ignored the brooding silence of the other two lieutenants, Ivar and Cormac. The two males didn't concern me. Ivar, like Blade, preferred action to strategy, wildness to self-discipline. He kept his black hair long enough to please the females, his pale blue eyes and wicked tongue—both in bed and out, if rumors were to be believed—kept him in a steady supply of their company. He was content to fight and leave the politics and strategy to me.

Ivar would follow Cormac's lead. And Cormac was mine. Through and through. And thank the gods for that. He was huge, a brute even by Hyperion standards, perhaps a bit closer to our ancestral bloodline than the rest of us. A full head taller than I, his black hair was streaked with silver at the temples, not from age, but from mixed blood, one of his ancestors having been from Silver and Blade's animal line. He'd been found as an infant, abandoned on the surface, perhaps too alien for the wild Hyperion mother who'd given birth to him to accept.

One of the Styx females had found him, raised him, trained him to fight.

My mother.

He was my brother in all the ways that counted and would never betray me.

But it was the captains who stood lining the walls of the small room who made the animal in me nervous. They raised their voices, arguing amongst themselves, thinking out loud. They were younger, volatile and somewhat unpredictable when compared to my battle-hardened lieutenants. Rash thinking kept them in junior positions until they had experience and wisdom to be anything more.

Blade was bringing our mate here. Was, in fact, already on his way. And I would not have her walk into danger. Nor would I tolerate any hint of disrespect.

She was mine. Which meant she was theirs now as well.

Their Lady Styx. Second only to me in our legion. I was asking them to kill for her. Die for her.

And I hadn't even claimed her yet. Gods, she had yet to *agree* to the claiming. I could fuck her, bite her and be done with it. But I would have her consent. I would have her willing.

My decision was made. The Hyperion in me would not relent. It took an act of will to keep my fangs from bursting free of my mouth in a show for dominance with every thought of her.

"She's Coalition, Styx. Are you sure this is the wisest course of action?" That was Silver, and immediately the captains' voices quieted. I appreciated her wisdom on allowing them to vent their frustration and concern before taking up their cause in a more rational, controlled tone of voice.

One that wouldn't get her killed.

I leaned forward, my fists resting on the top of the stone slab and let the smell of the home world calm my senses. Until I thought of laying Harper out on this table, filling her with my hard length, tasting her flesh with the scent of home surrounding us. I would never see this table, this room in the same way again.

Taking a deep breath, I ignored the ache of my hard cock and opened my eyes. "She is mine. My mate. Blade has agreed, and we will claim her together as soon as possible. As for Cerberus and whatever they were doing in the Latiri Star Cluster, we'll find out."

"Gods, Styx, have you lost your fucking mind?" Ivar blurted, running his hand through his black hair. "While I agree we need to know what Cerberus is doing, they've always been bad. It's nothing new. But her?"

I growled at the way he used that one word. *Her.* As if it tasted bad.

"She's an officer of the Coalition Fleet."

This was repeated again and again. She was Coalition. Not quite the enemy, but damned close.

"She's mine."

Silver raised a brow and leaned back, tipping her chair on one leg to rock back and forth, tempting gravity to take her down. "Technically, she's not yours, she belongs to *them.*"

I snarled at her, didn't try to hide my fangs this time. She held her hands out in front of herself to placate me. "I'm not trying to defy you, just pointing out the facts. Do you have a plan? A way to get her out of their system? Strip her from the Coalition database?"

"Yes." I did. It was risky, and I'd owe a favor to a scheming Prillon warrior I did not want to be indebted to any further, but nothing would stop me from keeping Harper. Nothing.

"Well?" Ivar asked, eyes wide, waiting. "What's the plan? What are we going to do about Cerberus? They'll bring the Coalition down on all of us."

"We could take them out." Cormac's deep, rumbling voice filled the small room, and an almost eerie silence descended on the group. It was not often a top level enforcer of Styx spoke of all out war with another legion. He pulled a blade from somewhere on his body, one of many he always carried, and watched the play of light on metal as he tilted it in the light. "One night. That's all I need, Styx. Give me enough from the coffers to hire some of those deserters from Everis. Some real Hunters. Astra legion might help as well. She hates Cerberus."

Silver choked on a small laugh. "That's because Cerberus wanted her for his mate." She settled her chair back on all four legs and grinned. "And Astra isn't too fond of males who don't know how to take no for an answer."

"He didn't want her, he wanted power. He wanted Astra legion." Khon spoke true, his green eyes narrowed beneath dark brows as he looked at Silver. "And that was twenty years ago."

Silver shrugged. "A woman never forgets."

"Gods know that's the fucking truth." Ivar grinned and a few of the captains around the room chuckled. If anyone understood the working of the female mind, it was Ivar. Perhaps that was another reason he was so skilled at luring unmated females into his bed. He had yet to find his mate. None of them in the room had.

"We will find the truth. Ivar, put men on it. Use the Everians if needed. I am willing to pay for a Hunter. Just find out what the fuck is going on."

At his nod, the door slid open and there she was.

Every eye turned to watch as my mate was escorted into the room by Blade. The sight of her, golden hair falling in a gleaming wave past her shoulders, her green eyes, bright as gemstones, assessing everyone in the room.

She wore the black uniform of Rogue 5 and the tight material hugged every luscious curve. The silver band around her arm made me want to beat my chest and roar to the heavens that she was mine. Mine. *Mine.*

Head high, her gaze locked on me, and I held out my hand to her. Blade walked in behind her and took his seat next to Silver, a look of contentment on his face I'd rarely seen. The usual tension was gone, the wildness somewhat tamed. Apparently, caring for our mate agreed with him.

It agreed with her as well. She was no longer stained with dirt and blood, the fear and weariness in her eyes now gone. And she wore our uniform. Our colors.

Ivar devoured my mate with his eyes, and I pulled her behind me, blocking his view, and growled a warning, to which he dropped his gaze and glanced at Silver for help. But Silver was even more interested in my mate than the males in the room. About a third of my officers were female, and their curiosity about the Earthling who had accomplished what none of them could—gain my interest, my devotion—was palpable.

I led Harper to the only open seat at the table—mine—and held it out for her. Reluctant to give up the tactile pleasure of holding her hand, I kept it in my own once she was settled and took my place behind her. Protector and guardian. She sat at the head of Styx legion, and I stood behind her. It was an important moment. I may have said she was mine, that she was my mate, a dozen times. Two dozen. Actions spoke louder than words, and the sight of her before me didn't need to be repeated.

It was as if my captains stopped breathing.

Only now did they understand how serious I was. How far I was willing to go. For her. My mate.

"Gods, Styx. You can't be serious." Ivar reeled in shock. I saw the confusion on his face. I'd never hinted at claiming a mate, honoring a female in such a way before. Giving her my seat at the table was the greatest honor I could give her, and she was completely unaware of the magnitude of my action. But my people were not.

Sensing the unrest in the room, Blade moved around the table to stand behind her opposite shoulder. "She is our mate. We will kill for her, die for her, and we ask you to do the same."

"She's Coalition," Silver said again, repeating her earlier statement. "She's a danger to us."

I saw my mate raise one pale brow, cross her arms over her ample breasts.

"And the mercenaries that took my MedRec team? They weren't Coalition. They were yours. They were *Legion.*" She lifted a hand and tapped her biceps where the silver stripe was. "Dressed like you, but with red. Here." She tilted her head to the side and glance up at me out of the corner of her eye. "Are you sure my staying here is the *wisest course of action*?"

Even though she hadn't been in the room at the time, her words echoed Silver's when she'd spoken of Harper. It was as if my mate thought we couldn't keep her safe.

Everyone started talking then, arguing about the presence of my mate.

As if it were up for debate.

"Enough!" I shouted.

Silence fell, only ragged breathing filled the room, everyone riled not only because I was taking an Earth mate, a Coalition member as my own, but because they were unsettled about news of Cerberus. A tenuous balance had been broken and the future was unclear. We were used to chaos, but not within our ranks.

"She is mine," I bit out through clenched teeth, daring anyone to argue further.

"What?" Harper protested, tried to rise, but I placed my hand on her shoulder and squeezed gently before moving to wrap it around her neck. I did not squeeze. The move was a caress, a display of intimacy, of trust between us. She leaned back, lifted her face toward me, not only accepting of my touch, but exposing her throat even more.

Silver's eyes narrowed thoughtfully, but my other enforcers visibly relaxed, fully understanding, in that one small gesture between male and female, what was already between us. They witnessed her beautiful submission. And that was all it took to see the truth of it all. She wasn't here for Coalition purposes. We weren't claiming her because we wanted an ally. No, they could all see that she really did belong to us.

"Styx? Blade? What are you doing?" Harper blinked up at me, confusion in her gaze.

"Claiming you."

She shook her head and looked back at the enforcers seated around the table before scanning the rest of the captains in the room. They all looked back at her without blinking, giving her their complete attention. Which, apparently, made my sweet mate uncomfortable because her back stiffened, her relaxed, calm attitude now slightly ruffled. "We need to talk about this, don't you think?" She glanced from me to Blade to Silver. "In private."

"No." Silver spoke and held my mate's gaze steady across the expanse of stone. "If you are his, I will fight for you, protect you, die for you, But, he must prove it beyond all doubt."

A knock at the door sounded, and I signaled the closest captain to allow our visitor entry.

Silver gasped when she saw him.

He had no name now, not since he'd taken his role as elder and advisor, wielder of the ink that marked us all. He had his supplies with him as I'd requested, everything Blade and I would need to banish all doubt from everyone present. If Silver wanted proof, the others would, too.

"Scribe. Thank you for coming."

"Of course." He bowed slightly at the waist, and the others, my enforcers included, rose to bow back to him. He was old, he'd been an old man when I was a boy and no one remembered his given name. He inked the names of new babes and members of my legion on my flesh, officiated at all matings. He was our record keeper, historian and my personal council. And he was here at my command.

He carried his small black bag under his arm. Within that bag? Ink. Silver bolts. Everything he'd need to send me down an unchangeable path.

I yanked my shirt over my head, and Harper turned at the motion, her eyes going wide with desire as she studied me, her attention lingering on the lines of names inked into my flesh with a fascination I was eager to test. She had never seen my bare chest before.

"What's going on? What are you doing?" she asked.

Cormac grinned, the first time I'd seen the look on his face in recent memory.

When Blade pulled off his shirt as well, the shuffling and whispers in the room ceased and Scribe placed his bag on the table next to my mate. "You sure about this, Styx? What's done cannot be undone." His official words were for me this time, the only warning I'd receive from him. Blade, too. This was permanent. Forever.

I looked down at my beautiful mate, took her scent into my lungs and stopped trying to control the fangs that ached to sink into her flesh, marking her, claiming her, driving her into a mating frenzy. Blade had been gifted with a taste of her sweet pussy on Zenith. Soon I would taste her. Fuck her.

Claim her. Forever. My mouth watered and my cock ached to do so.

"I'm sure. She is mine. I honor her claim and accept her mark."

"What mark? What are you talking about?" Harper looked from me to Blade, confused. But Blade lifted his hand to her opposite shoulder and repeated my earlier words.

"She is my mate. I honor her claim and accept her mark."

"Would someone tell me what the hell is going on?" Harper scowled at both of us, the irritated look of a woman thwarted by her men. I smiled back as Scribe took his ink from the bag.

"Where shall her mark be placed?" he asked.

I'd saved space, high on my chest, at the base of my neck where even a uniform wouldn't hide her name from my legion, a spot for my future mate's name to be prominently placed. I put my finger to the spot. "Here, Scribe. Her name is Harper."

I placed my hands on the table, bent at the waist so he could reach.

He nodded in approval and got to work. First, I looked at each person around the table, silently telling them this was done. It was official. Then I looked at Harper. Didn't look away.

The needle and ink went deep, the pain part of my test of loyalty. I wished in that moment her name was longer, the burn and everything it stood for making my balls ache, my entire body hum with barely suppressed need.

Those assembled watched in silence as he finished with me and went through the same process with Blade. Harper's gaze drifting back and forth in fascination, and not a little desire. Her attention lingered, and as Scribe worked on Blade, she raised her fingers to my flesh, traced her name with trembling hands. "Why? Why did you do this?"

I took her hand and pressed it over her name, forever etched in my body. "Because you are mine and I am yours."

Her stunned look made me want to kiss her, but she turned from me and looked at Blade. He spoke over Scribe's bent head. "You are mine, Harper, and I am yours."

"Holy shit." She stared, shocked perhaps? Trembling. A little pale. I looked to Blade.

"Did you feed her?" I snarled.

"Of course," Blade barked right back and Silver laughed.

"By the gods, this is going to be fun to watch." She leaned back in her chair, arms crossed and put her feet up on the stone slab with a grin on her face.

"I'm right here, you know," Harper countered. "And I'm not a pet. I'm an intelligent adult. I am perfectly capable of taking care of myself."

"No."

"No."

Blade and I denied her claim at the exact same time and Ivar grinned, glancing at Silver. "Fun? Nothing like seeing our two best fighters get their balls chopped off."

A hint of laughter came from the captains lining the room, standing along the walls, watching with rapt attention the show we were putting on.

This claiming would be talked about for years. Being here, in this moment, was an honor they would tell their grandchildren about.

When the inking was done, Scribe pulled two silver bars from his bag, a question in his old eyes.

"Yes," I said in response. "In the old way."

Blade nodded and we stood steady as Scribe pierced our nipples with the bars, the mark of a mated male, one well claimed.

Harper sputtered and tried to intervene once she figured out what was happening. "What...why—"

"More proof. Ownership. You *own* us, Harper. We are yours, mate."

I said nothing more and thankfully, she fell silent. If she had questions, I would explain them. Later.

I didn't even flinch at the bright stab of pain once and then again. The piercings could not be removed, not without tearing the flesh. They were a sign of our faithfulness, our loyalty to one female. Our mate. We would touch no other. Allow no other female to touch us.

Harper winced in sympathy as the sharp metal pierced my flesh, but I welcomed the burn. The pain. It was how I knew she was mine. Now and forever.

Finally, after what felt like hours, the old man was finished. He stepped back to admire his work. Blade and I a matching pair with Harper's name swirling in our flesh and silver bars proclaiming us as hers.

"It is done," he said.

"Yes, it is done." I looked around the room, met every pair of eyes. There were no more questions, no more doubts. Harper was mine and every enforcer and captain in the room knew exactly how serious I was about keeping her. "Harper is mine. I have chosen Blade as a bond-mate, to help care for her and protect her. Harper is Styx. Welcome her."

The enforcers stood again and everyone in the room bowed, including Blade and Scribe as I stood behind her, ready to kill anyone who questioned her or showed her disrespect.

None dared.

Blade lifted his head to me, an eager grin on his face. "Enough?" he asked.

"Enough," I agreed and raised my voice to one of command. "Now, everyone, get the fuck out."

Harper jumped in her seat, something suspiciously like tears in her eyes as she looked at everyone bowing to her. She tried to rise and follow the others, but I held her in place with my hand on her shoulder.

"Not you, mate." When she turned to look up at me with a question in her eyes, I let her see what I'd been holding back—raging hunger. Need. Lust. "It's my turn to taste you."

$\mathcal{H}$ *arper*

HOLY. SHIT.

I wasn't in Kansas anymore, Toto. No. I wasn't even on Zenith. I knew Styx and Blade were wild, but...wow. Not *this* wild. I shrugged out of Styx's hold and rose, pacing the room to release some of the pent up tension. I placed the giant stone table between us and watched them as their gazes locked on me. They stood opposite me, bare chests rising and falling with their heavy breaths.

Their chests.

Broad. Hard. Washboard abs. Narrow waists. *Tattoos.* Not a simple anchor on a pec or even a rose and barbed wire with a name entwined. No. They were covered with black words. Not words. Names. Styx was covered, the entire legion of names written on his perfect skin. Blade's body held fewer names, as I suspected the rest of the enforcers' bodies did as well. But on these two, my name was prominently placed on their chests. The letters larger than the rest. Their intention obvious. Not exactly an engagement ring, but...damn. So hot. Their lack of doubt, their absolute conviction that I was the one they wanted was wearing me down, making me want to believe them.

Making me want to be claimed. Fucked.

Bitten.

And then there were the piercings. I'd seen pictures of guys with their nipples pierced. Some rings, some bars like they had. Blade and Styx were light and dark. Huge. Alien. Their stoic welcome for the needle that inked my name into their bodies—permanently—made my pussy hot and swollen. They were strong. Determined. Ripped—with muscles bulging everywhere. They looked too good to be real and seeing my name on them, *my claim* forever etched into their skin? My panties were completely and totally ruined.

They'd fought their core group of leadership for me. Not physically, but I knew it would come to that if necessary. They'd gotten my name tattooed on them and then their nipples pierced to prove I was their mate. The woman they *chose.* Me. Out of all the women in the galaxy, all the Coalition worlds, and all the worlds like this one that lived on the fringes. They chose me. My gaze lingered on the silver bars, on their version of a wedding ring, and my own nipples hardened and tingled at the thought.

"Why didn't you bite me like they wanted?" I asked, as if the other stuff wasn't enough.

Both men were staring at me as if I were a little baby bunny and they were ravenous wolves. No, they weren't

84

wolves. They were like vampires, ready to bite me, to claim me. Mark me as theirs.

"As I said, you are our mate, but you are not ready to be claimed," Styx said. The spot where my name was inked into his chest was red, irritated from the needle. As a healer, I wanted to pull out a wand and take away the pain, but I doubted he even felt it. And maybe I wanted him to feel it, just for a few minutes. I wanted to be the reason his chest burned. I wanted to mark them both. Wanted them to know they belonged to me.

The thought was savage and instinctive, a thought no educated woman should have, but there it was anyway. My pulse pounded, and my breasts grew sensitive and heavy with the possessive, primitive thoughts. Maybe I was turning into an animal here. Maybe it was in the freaking water, making me as wild as they were.

"Then why am I here?" I asked. The large table was between us, but it was no impediment if they wanted me. They were holding back. They'd held back with the others, too, but I sensed a difference now. A coiled gentleness.

Odd, yes, but I knew instinctively they wouldn't hurt me. They'd protected me from their fellow Styx members. They'd killed the attacker on the transport pad, argued and bargained with a Prillon officer. They wouldn't hurt me.

"Because you are our mate," Blade said. They kept repeating the words, but my mind continued to rebel. Logic refused to accept that forever was this easy. That two males, as gorgeous as they were, would want a registered nurse from Los Angeles who wasn't from their world. It didn't make sense.

"But I'm not one of you." I pointed to the now closed door. "They made that point very clear."

Styx put his hand to my name, now permanently embedded in his skin. "You are one of us now. They know it. They witnessed your name inked into our flesh, the piercings. There is no doubt. Soon, everyone will know." He came around the table, his eyes squarely on mine. If a singing leprechaun came dancing into the room, I doubted he'd glance away.

"But what about my team? The mercenaries? I can't just stay here on Rogue 5 and belong to you. I need to find them, to save them."

"I agree they need to be found, those who did it brought to justice, but not by you. You are a healer, Harper, not a warrior. Leave this to us. We have contacts within the Fleet. Your people are not forgotten. Trust us. Let us take care of it. Tracking our enemies is not safe for you."

"Why not? I can go back to Zenith. I would have an entire battalion there keeping me safe." There were plenty of Coalition fighters in the Latiri system, more than enough warriors on Zenith to protect me. Hell, if I had to, I could ask to be moved to a medical station on Battleship Karter.

"They don't know who this enemy is. We do," Styx countered.

"And that makes me safer, being closer to the enemy?" I sighed, feeling like I was hitting my head against a wall.

Styx straightened to his full height, his bare chest expanding as he stared me down. A move to intimidate, but all it did was make me want to touch. Learn. Taste. "How did they know your team was going to be on that planet? How did they know exactly where you were? And when?"

Those questions had been hovering in the back of my mind, but the only potential answers were terrible. Horrible. My mind refused to accept them. "No." It was all I could say.

"Yes, Harper. You know the truth. There is a traitor among your people. Someone told them where you would be. How many guards would be with you. Exactly where to land. You were betrayed."

"No. That's impossible." I shook my head and took a step back, but I wasn't convincing anyone, especially not myself.

"You are safer here, with your mates," Blade added. "Ivar has been assigned to discover the truth. To find the scavengers from Rogue 5 who did this to your team and finish them."

"What about my team?" The thought of them dead or turned into Hive made me nauseated. "Where are they? I can't just forget about them. We have to find them."

"Ivar will find them, too. Rescue them. I have given him permission to contract with the Everian Elite Hunters for help," Styx added. "None of the warriors will be restricted by following Coalition protocol. They will do what needs to be done to end this. No matter what it takes."

I'd met some Hunters, knew their abilities. And based on what I knew of Styx members, they didn't like following rules. Maybe it would help if they didn't have bureaucratic bullshit to deal with. God knew the government and military back home moved a lot faster when a team of SEALS went in than when something got buried in a bureaucratic committee. "Okay. But I'm just supposed to stay here and do...what, in the meantime? Twiddle my thumbs? Wait for the Coalition to track me down and send me to military prison for desertion?"

"There will be no prison, mate," Blade said. "We will take care of that as well."

"How?" Even if I wanted to stay with these two, I just couldn't see a way out of this mess. "I don't want to be an outlaw. I'm not—that's just not—I can't live like that." I knew myself well enough to know that I didn't operate that way. If I gave my word, I kept it. I didn't break the law. I didn't rebel. I was a healer, not a fighter. And I'd signed a contract. I had pledged to serve Earth out here, pledged to help. At least for a while longer. Two more months. I'd planned to sign up for another two years. But I could change plans. I could not live with becoming a deserter. A liar. How many human warriors would die out there because I wasn't there to help?

"You will learn to trust us, mate." Styx's voice brooked no argument, and since I didn't see a way out of any of this at the moment, I let it go and hoped like hell Styx and Blade knew what they were talking about. I wanted to trust them. I wanted everything they told me to be true. They were dangling happily-ever-after in front of me and, like a lovesick fool, I wanted to run toward it.

"We will take care of you, Harper. In *every* way." Blade's deep voice, his intense gaze, did more to me than any kind of foreplay with a guy from Earth.

"You know who you belong to." Styx's gaze darted to the base of my neck, where I was sure my pulse was racing at a thundering gallop beneath my skin. "Your body knows."

I slowly shook my head. "You have to bite me, don't you?" I put my hand to my neck. "They wanted you to do it here. Now. They wanted to watch."

Styx closed the distance between us. Growled. I refused to retreat. "They will not witness such an intimate act. When we bite you, when we inject our mating serum into your flesh, it is a very personal act. I refuse to share it."

Blade moved and joined us so I was between the two of them, one on either side of me. I felt small, sheltered. Protected after such a confrontation.

88

"Will you turn me?"

Styx frowned. "Turn you?" He spun me about so I faced him. He tilted my chin up with his fingers. Blade's hands settled on my shoulders. "Like this?"

I couldn't help but smile. "No, I meant your bite. Will it turn me into something else? Like a vampire who can't go out into the sun?"

Blade's thumbs caressed the back of my neck. His touch was so gentle in comparison to his angry argument just a short time ago. "They have these vampires on Earth? Why would you not be able to go into the sun?"

I shook my head. "No. They're not real. They are just stories. But the vampires are immortal as long as they stay in the dark. They have fangs, like yours." I smiled as Styx opened his mouth just enough to flash his fangs at me.

"Not like mine." He leaned in until our noses touched. "Mine will light your body on fire. Our bite will make you come over and over as we fuck you."

Did my knees just wobble? Because holy shit, these two were hot. But I still needed to know more about this biting thing. "A vampire is incredibly strong and fast. They survive on human blood, but they have one major weakness. They will die in sunlight." As I explained more about vampires, Styx's dark eyebrows went up, then the corner of his mouth twitched. "If a vampire bites a human, the human becomes one of them."

"We are not like your vampires," Styx said. "Our bite will not change who or what you are. We are strong and fast, but we are not immortal. Our bite has a mating serum in it. When it seeps into your flesh, it affects your cells, but not in the way you mentioned. You will not become what we are."

Blade brushed my hair to the side so he could kiss the

side of my neck. "Your senses will become heightened, every part of you will be totally and completely alive. You will feel the smallest touch, your body so sensitive, so aware, that the ridges of our cocks will make you whimper and beg and scream as we fill you." His lips lingered and the top of his fangs brushed over my skin in a deliberate tease. "You will crave our touch, and we will crave you."

"Just as I crave you now," Styx added. "I only had your taste on my fingers before, and I want more. Need it."

I remembered Blade on his knees in the hallway at Zenith station, the skilled attention of his tongue, how Styx had fucked me with his fingers first. Licked them. Oh yes, that had been so good.

"So you'll bite me? Now?" I asked, a touch apprehensive. If it meant more orgasms like the ones they'd given me in that hallway, I just might consider it. Had that only been a few hours ago? But I wasn't an idiot, and there was more at stake here than whatever was between us. "What about the Coalition? They'll look for me eventually. What happens if I don't return to my post? I've got two months left on my service contract. I can't just not go back."

Styx shook his head, studied my lips. "I know, Harper. We will address these issues. I promise you, all will be well. And we won't bite you until you are ready to be claimed. I promise, mate, that when you are ready, you will beg us for it."

"The others know you belong to us," Blade added. "The piercings alone prove to the entire legion exactly what you mean to us. They are the outward sign that we are yours. Just as the scars from our bite—when the time comes—will be our visible mark upon you."

I glanced down at Styx's chest, the silver posts that

disappeared through each of his nipples, the flesh red and angry from the injury. I wanted to lift my hand, touch the small bar, flick it with my finger. No, I wanted to suck on them and watch his reaction, flick the sensitive area with my tongue, but I didn't dare. "Don't they hurt?"

"I embrace the pain, mate. It reminds me that you are here with us, that you are ours."

"I don't want my nipples pierced. Do I have to do that, too?" I was afraid of the answer. I didn't need the old man coming back and doing the same to me.

Styx grinned then as he slowly shook his head. "No one will touch those breasts but us. No one will cause you pain. Not while you're mine." His eyes narrowed, full-on alpha male issuing a proclamation like everything he said was law. And, yeah, I felt like that helpless bunny once more, facing a hungry wolf. Prey. I was prey. But I didn't want to run. I wanted to be caught.

"The bite will come later. For now, we will remind you that we are your mates by pleasuring you." Styx's voice dropped an octave, and the sound of it had me shivering.

"Oh," I said. I liked that idea much better than a nipple piercing.

"It is my turn to taste you."

I barely frowned my confusion when Styx lifted me up and placed me on the edge of the table. With a hand on my chest, he pushed me back so I was lying down on the hard surface.

"Styx?" I asked.

Each guy grabbed one of my feet, worked off a shoe, dropped it to the floor. Together, they tugged off my pants.

Blade growled as he fought the material down my legs. "No more pants for you. We need easy access to your pussy."

"I can't go around half naked!" I protested, although I wasn't putting up any kind of fight as they placed my feet on the edge of the table, intentionally very far apart. My pussy was completely open and on display. They could miss *nothing*.

"Of course not," Styx said, as he pushed a chair out of his way, his eyes on mine. "We won't let you out of our quarters."

He dropped to his knees, and I had to come up onto my elbows to see him. Both of them had a hand still on the top of each of my feet.

"I'm not in your quarters now," I countered, stating the obvious.

"I want your flavor on my tongue." His free hand slid up the inside of my bare thigh, brushed over the eager folds of my pussy. "Your scream ringing in my ears."

"My scream?" I asked, arching my back as he learned me with his fingertips.

"Oh, you'll scream. I won't let you up until you do."

Styx's words were a promise, and I lowered myself back to the cold stone as he put his mouth on me and proved it.

He had me writhing in a matter of seconds, my hips rising into his every lick.

"I told you she was sweet," Blade said. "Sensitive."

Styx growled as he sucked on my clit and slipped a finger into me.

"Oh god," I moaned.

I was wet. I could feel it, and I was sure Styx could taste it. The sound of his mouth on me filled the room. I tried to grip the table, but I had no purchase, my fingers sweaty.

Styx lifted his head, and I cried out.

"Shh," Blade soothed, his calloused hand sliding up and down my calf. "He'll take care of you."

I believed him, but I wasn't sure if I would survive. I'd been so close to coming when Styx pulled away. The bastard.

But when he slipped his thumb into my pussy, I felt something pressing against my bottom. A slick finger.

"Styx!" I cried out.

"You said you've been with two men," he said, his voice coming from between my spread thighs. "Ever been taken here?"

His finger circled, then pressed in, gently yet insistently. My body instinctively resisted, but it also knew the pleasure to be had and relented, the digit sliding in up to the first knuckle.

I nodded my head as I clenched down.

"Good, then you won't need to be trained."

Blade's palm squeezed my leg, and Styx lowered his head, taking my clit into his mouth and giving it firm suction.

This wasn't Styx getting a taste of me. This was an all-out assault. I couldn't hold anything back, the pleasure too great. His tongue was skilled on my clit, his finger and thumb sliding in and out in an alternating motion that mimicked what they would do with their cocks. They'd claim me together, and they knew I'd done it before. In college, I'd paired up with a couple of guys who were roommates in my dorm. We'd had some fun together, enough that the thought of sharing Styx and Blade that way nearly overloaded my system.

I liked what he was doing to me right now. Not liked it. *Loved* it. I couldn't hold back. Styx wouldn't let me.

My body coiled tight, my skin heated, my mind completely blank. The pleasure overwhelmed, coalesced and burst. I came on a scream. Hard. So hard that I saw white behind my eyelids. My fingers and toes tingled.

Once wasn't enough for them it seemed because while Styx eased up on his attentions while I came, he didn't stop. In fact, the second I exhaled and slumped on the table, he revived his assault. I came again, almost instantly.

Then again.

Only when I was a sweaty, wilted mess did he stand up, pull me from the table and toss me over his shoulder.

"Styx! Where are you taking me?" I asked, feeling the cool air on my swollen, very wet pussy.

"Our quarters to fuck you."

"People will see," I replied. I was barely coherent after the overload of pleasure, but I knew I didn't want to be shared. Or carried bare ass naked through the hallway.

"Our personal quarters are attached," he countered. It was only then I paid enough attention to notice we weren't going out the door I'd entered with Blade, but through a different one I hadn't noticed before.

"Why didn't we come into the meeting this way?" I asked Blade.

Styx slapped my bare bottom playfully, the sting adding to the bursting excess of sensation running through my body. "These are our private quarters. No one sees inside. Anyone but you, I or Blade enters without permission, it's a death sentence."

"What?" Was he kidding me? "That's crazy." I was tossed down on a bed, bounced once and they were upon me. My shirt was off, my bra gone before I could even organize my thoughts.

94

"That's Styx." Blade was grinning. "He likes his privacy." He bent down and sucked my nipple into his mouth, just for a moment, before releasing the sensitive peak. The action almost like a hello. "I thought he was overzealous, but I find now that I agree. I don't like the idea of anyone entering our quarters with you here. Naked. In our bed."

"Where we intend to keep you." Styx stood at the end of the bed, his hungry gaze devouring every naked inch of me. "Perfect. Just where we want you."

The bed was big, plush and black. I'd barely caught a glimpse of the living area as he carried me through it. Dark furniture, thick and piled with pillows. I got a sense of comfort, lavish attention paid to the details. Just like in this room.

While everything about Styx screamed hard, judgmental, efficient, everything around me seemed to be the opposite. Soft. Luxurious. Welcoming. If Styx's persona was the hard candy coating, his personal space was the soft, melted caramel of my new favorite treat.

8

I'D NEVER BEEN SO HARD IN MY LIFE. OUR MATE WAS PERFECT. Gorgeous. Brave. Passionate. Eager. Cautious.

Different.

And the fact that she cared for her MedRec team had me respecting her more. But if she thought she would be the one who would go after them, to find them and face Cerberus and whatever fucked-up plans they had, she was very, very wrong.

Ivar and the Hunters would find out the truth. We just had to stay out of their way and let them do what they were good at. In the meantime, we would learn everything there was to learn about Harper.

She wasn't like any potential Hyperion mate. She wasn't even like Katie, the only other female I'd encountered from

Earth. Katie had been a virgin, inexperienced and unclaimed. Her mate, Bryn, would have had to teach her pleasure slowly, walk a fine line between seduction and fear.

I did not want to hold back. I did not want to be careful. I wanted to devour our mate. Feast on her. Push her limits. See just how far she could go without shattering with orgasm. As ideas flooded my mind, images of our mate in various positions, writhing and wet and taking us both, I was grateful to the gods themselves that Harper was not a virgin.

Not at all. I knew some who wanted innocence, who wanted to be the first to open up his mate's pussy, who were envious of past lovers, jealousy their constant companion. I internally shrugged at the idea. Any Earthling Harper had been with was just practice for her. They meant nothing. They *were* nothing because they weren't me and Styx.

She was experienced, but she had never come so easily or so beautifully for any of the lovers in her past. I had no proof, but I knew nonetheless.

Harper was ours. Because she'd been with two men before, her ass had been prepared. She knew what it would be like to be with us—at least in concept. Reality with Styx and I would be completely different.

We didn't have to hold back, to be gentle when we knew she wanted rough. We could be bold, explore the depth of her submission without managing the anxiety or uncertainty of a mild, fearful virgin.

We weren't tame. We weren't the males to introduce a female to fucking.

No. We'd eaten Harper out, made her come, but we'd yet to fuck her. In the proverbial buffet of sexual options, we'd only had an appetizer.

The way she looked up at us from Styx's bed, naked and eager, there was no doubt she wanted more as much as we did. She was small, over a head shorter than either of us. Her pale skin blushed a pretty pink from her cheeks and neck up over the swells of her breasts. And her breasts?

Fuck.

Lush and a perfect handful. I knew since I'd cupped them in my palms while in the hallway of the canteen, but that had been over her uniform. Now, they were bare, and I could see her dark pink nipples, tightly furrowed. They were begging to be played with, to be pinched, sucked, licked and even clamped. She wasn't solid muscle, hard like many Hyperion women, all bones and angles. No, she had soft curves, a belly that was slightly rounded, hips full and wide. And an ass that would perfectly cushion my hips as I took her there.

I groaned thinking about spanking it, seeing my handprint bloom. To take her from behind, to fuck her pussy as I gripped her hips. To claim that readied ass.

"Do you trust us to pleasure you?" I asked, removing my comm unit from my wrist, tossing it onto a nearby table. My patience—albeit meager as I'd watched Styx have his turn at her pussy—was gone.

My balls ached to sink into her. My palms itched to feel her soft, heated skin.

She looked up at me, her lips parted, her green eyes wide with a mix of desire and eagerness. She knew we weren't done, even though she'd come three times.

"Yes," she said, coming up onto her knees, her eyes on my chest.

The piercings throbbed, but not as much as my cock.

"I...I want to touch you."

I put my hands out to my sides, grinned. "I'm all yours."

Styx laughed, toed off his boots. "Don't worry, mate. You can have your way with us. Any way you want."

"I have no idea why, but I want to put my mouth on your piercings," she admitted, and my cock pulsed against my pants. "They're so damn hot, but I'm a healer. I don't want them to get infected."

Styx went over to a wall unit, opened one of the doors and pulled out a ReGen wand. The blue light came on and he waved it over one piercing, then the other, before tossing it to me to use next. It took only seconds to heal the minor tissue damage.

"There. All healed." He walked to the edge of the bed and dropped down, turning to his back with his head on the pillows. His legs were bent and his feet hung off the side so not to bump Harper. "Have at us."

When I was done, I dropped the wand beside my comm unit and came to stand at the foot of the bed, just out of her reach. I kept my hands at my sides. Waited.

She glanced over her shoulder at Styx, then at me. She chose me to be first, perhaps because I was closer, and crawled over so she could flick her tongue against the embedded metal.

It was almost impossible to keep from grabbing her and tossing her onto the bed beside Styx and fucking her.

"Like them?"

Her hands came to rest on my chest to give herself balance. She moaned, and I felt it all the way to my balls.

"I had no idea piercings on a guy could be so hot," she murmured.

Her mouth was soft and wet, her tongue flicking out and

she even tugged. When she switched to the other piercing, I let her have a few seconds of play and that was it. I grabbed her hips, tossed her onto the bed.

She bounced, and I reveled in the way her breasts swayed and her legs fell open.

Styx took the opportunity to pounce, climbing on top of her and kissing her, stifling her cry of surprise. His knee nudged hers apart, opening her up so his hips could settle between her parted thighs.

He kissed along her jaw, down her neck, even grazing his teeth over the spot where he would someday soon bite her, on his way down to her nipples.

"We like nipples, too," he said before taking one hard tip into his mouth. He tugged and pulled it taut.

I watched her back arch and her fingers tangle in his hair as I shucked my boots and pants. My cock bobbed toward her as if it knew exactly what it wanted.

Harper.

"I thought...I thought I could have my way with you," she replied, her voice breathy, her eyes slipping closed.

Styx lifted himself up onto his hands, looming over her. "If you can still think, we're not doing it right."

I sat down on the side of the bed, tucked my hands under her arms and lifted her up. Styx shifted, allowing me to pull her so she was resting against me, my front to her back. She settled between my parted legs, my cock nestled against her back.

"This is going to be fast, mate. One of these days, when we're not so desperate to sink into your tight body, we'll let you be in charge."

I laughed at his statement, even as I hooked my foot over

her ankle, nudged her wider. "We'll always be desperate to sink into you. Pussy or ass," I replied, curling my hips so she felt the hard swell of my cock.

She whimpered as Styx moved closer and settled between her thighs, gripped the base of his cock and slid it through her swollen folds.

"Or mouth," Styx added. "Pussy first. Ready, mate?"

She nodded against my chest, her hair silky soft.

Styx didn't hesitate, only lined himself up and thrust deep in one stroke.

His eyes fell closed, and he groaned as his cock disappeared inside our mate. Harper arched her back and pressed her head against me. Gripping the back of one knee, I pulled it up and back, giving Styx more room.

He was braced on his hands and knees, fucking her. Hard. Her breasts swayed, soft cries of pleasure escaped her throat as he took her.

"So tight. So wet. Perfect," Styx said. Dark, dirty words as he pummeled her.

"Good?" I asked, my lips sliding over the curve of her ear.

"So good," she replied.

"Our mate likes it rough."

Styx grinned, but he was too lost in his own need to do more.

"You'll come, Harper," I commanded.

If she weren't being fucked, she'd probably give me an evil stare for being bossy, but I knew she liked it. Especially now when we were giving her exactly what she needed. She was safe between us, safe to feel what she wanted, to say what she wanted, to come. Even if it was wild and wet, dirty and hot as fuck.

She didn't scream this time. Instead, her breath was trapped, her body taut against mine as she came. Sweat bloomed on her skin, and we were slick together, the feel of her sliding over my new piercings making pre-cum seep from my cock and coat her back.

I imagined the feel of Harper's pussy milking Styx's cock as she came, finishing him. He came on a deep thrust and a growl. His fangs came out, and he angled his head back as he pumped into her.

They were both breathing hard, trying to recover as my cock continued to seep seed. I needed in her. Now.

Styx pulled out, and leaned back until his head rested on the pillows. He wrapped his arms around Harper and pulled her forward, off me so she straddled his body, on her hands and knees, looking down at him as I studied the perfect display from behind. From my position, I had the perfect view of her well used pussy, Styx's seed slipping from her swollen, cherry red lower lips. It wasn't that hole I was after, but the one above it, the one she'd had fucked before, prepared for us. For this moment. Leaning over, I grabbed the lube from the small table beside the bed. While I'd been seeing to Harper's bath and food, Styx had done more than just try to soothe our enforcers, the leaders within the legion.

"I love pussy, mate," I said, as I climbed onto the bed and positioned myself behind her. Opening the bottle of the slick fluid, my balls tightened to the point of agony. Anticipation was a blessing and a curse. Exquisite. Painful. "But I like ass, too. I'm going to fuck your other hole. If you've got objections, tell me now."

She looked over her shoulder at me as my lubed hand hovered over my cock.

Biting her lip, she eyed me, sizing me up and perhaps wondering if I'd fit. I would.

"You'll come from my cock in your ass. I promise."

I was cocky, sure. I also knew my mate, knew what she wanted. What she needed.

When she didn't respond, I gave her a playful swat to her round ass cheek.

She startled, making her breasts swing. "Yes?" I asked.

"Yes," she replied, lowering to her forearms, her chest pressed to Styx's as she left her ass high in the air. For me. An invitation.

Fuck.

Styx tangled his hands in her hair and kissed her, holding her in place, devouring her as I quickly coated my cock in the lube and used my slippery fingers to ring and coat her entrance. When I slipped a finger inside, I watched as she clenched the covers, gasped against Styx's lips.

Styx reached down and grabbed the rounded lobes of her ass, pulled them wide, opening her for me. She whimpered and claimed his mouth with her own, for the first time, the aggressor.

My balls drew up and I groaned. I wanted in. Now.

I removed my finger and aligned my cock to her entrance. Pressed.

I watched her hands, the line of her back, her breathing as I carefully opened her up. She was tight, but she knew to relax, to push back, and the flared crown of my cock slipped in. She stopped kissing Styx and arched her back. Sobbed.

"Finger her clit, Blade. Finger her clit and pull her head back. I want to taste her where our bite will mark her flesh." Styx's voice was rough, demanding as he slid his own hands up her body to tease her nipples, to tug and flick and play.

Doing as he ordered, I fisted one hand in her hair and gently tugged her head back and up, arching her spine, exposing her long, tender throat to Styx.

He leaned up, clamped his mouth down on her neck, not to bite, but to tease. Her ass clenched around my cock, so hard, so tight, I froze with a groan, afraid to move, afraid I'd lose control.

Reaching around with my free hand, I found her hard clit, gently flicked it with my finger as I began to move. In. Out. Deeper and deeper into her. This wasn't a hard fuck like Styx had given her pussy, but a slow glide. She clenched down like a vise. I wasn't going to last, but I was going to get balls deep before I filled her with my seed.

"So fucking perfect, Harper. You're taking me beautifully. Come for me and you'll take me with you."

In and out I moved, carefully, dripping more lube at the taut entrance, and I watched as I disappeared into her again and again.

My orgasm built at the base of my spine, curled my toes. My seed all but burst from my balls, and I gripped her hip, marking her with my tight hold as I marked her deep inside with my seed.

She was ours, pussy and ass. And when she came again, her head tossed back, her inner walls clenching and milking me deeper and deeper, her mouth open on a silent scream as Styx held her in place with his almost bite, I knew she held nothing back as well.

So much was against our match. We had a fight on our hands with enemies known and unknown.

But there was one constant now in our lives. One pleasure.

Harper.

———

Styx, One Week Later

"This is the price I have to pay to be Styx leader," I grumble, surveying the room before us.

While there were five legions on the moon base, there was one central legion-free area that was used for meetings. Not one legion had precedence. It was the only place that was neutral ground, where it was agreed no one ruled. But no leader—in current times—had taken a mate. Until now.

It was a given the event would occur here, in this large room. The central round table was removed so mingling could occur.

Mingling. I frowned just thinking the word. And looking around the space, so far there were about twenty enforcers from the various legions of Rogue 5. Half of them were mine, and I knew more would come.

Mingling. I would have to talk with those I didn't know and didn't care to, all for the sake of fucking protocol. This was one rule I would uphold.

We knew members of Cerberus had tried to kill Harper, and I wanted to study them. This event, this legion-neutral event was the perfect place. Every day Harper asked for an update on finding the mercenaries who took her MedRec team and her teammates whereabouts. Every day I had no answers. We had yet to hear from Ivar or the Hunters, and I was surprised. Cerberus was here on Rogue 5; they didn't need to travel far to find out the truth. But they *were* Hunters, and it proved the truth sometimes was hard to find.

To dig out. Maybe, just maybe, there was more to what happened than either Blade, Harper or I knew.

I wanted the truth, no matter how long it took. In the meantime, I had to keep my mate from climbing the walls in frustration, fear and worry. Distracting her with fucking seemed to work, but I didn't want to diminish what we did by making it that. A distraction.

And while Harper had been bothered before, it was my turn to want to climb the damn walls. I hated this fucking event, but it had to happen. Yet, I wanted to show off my new mate. To flaunt her, even. She was mine, she was perfect and no one else besides Blade would fucking have her.

"You like parties," Blade replied. If I didn't recognize the sarcasm in his words, I'd punch him in the face. Especially with the smirk I saw there now.

We stood to the side and watched everyone mingling and talking, although based on the colored arm bands that signified their legion, no one was intermixing.

We were the guests of honor, but Harper was the focus of everyone's attention. She the first mate of a legion leader who was not Hyperion for as long as anyone could remember. It was rare and a complete surprise. Hell, it was a complete surprise to me as well; I hadn't gone to Zenith for a mate, but by the gods, I'd left with one.

That she was an Earthling only added to the curiosity surrounding her.

I'd heard murmurs and rumors about how we'd found her. Why we'd chosen her—as if we'd had much choice. They also eyed her as if she were an outsider, which she was, but also noticed the lack of scars at the base of her neck indicating we had yet to officially claim her.

If any of the whispers of how we were going to use her and send her back to her planet got to our mate's ears, I would rip the speaker's tongue from his mouth. I knew of it all, but I refused to lower myself to argue. My words were nothing for proof. Only the bite of a mate, or mates, would shut down the damned lies.

She knew the reason we'd fucked her for the past week, but had yet to bite her. We'd told her before we'd even fucked her the first time, she would beg for the bite. Until then, we'd pleasure her, proving each time our desire for her. Our need.

Three from Astra arrived next, looked to me and Blade from the entrance, nodded. Then focused squarely on Harper who stood between us.

"You're not the ones everybody's ogling," Harper whispered, reaching down and grabbing my hand. I knew she was nervous, anxious even because of the attack on Zenith. That some of those with red arm bands were in the room. The fact that she was here, between us, proved her trust in us, that we'd protect her from harm. Even with our lives.

I recognized the heat in one of the male Astra's eyes when he gazed at my mate. Not that I could blame him, for she looked exceptionally beautiful. Her skin glowed. Her lips were full and swollen from many hours of kissing. She looked well-fucked, well-loved and glowing with happiness.

Blade tugged her into his side, pinning her in place with his arm about her waist, but she didn't let go of me as if she could sense the tension in the room.

These people were not my friends. There was a reason my enforcers were here, along with five of my captains. A breach in protocol they'd simply have to forgive.

I was not taking chances with Harper's safety. I'd known her only a week, had yet to be accepted fully by her. But already I knew losing her would destroy me.

9

Styx

"YOU ARE THE FIRST, MATE. YOU ARE THE REASON FOR THIS night," Blade told her, even though she knew this. The event had been planned once word spread of Harper's arrival on the moon base. While the legions were not friendly with each other, it was custom to introduce a new mate to the leaders and their underlings of each legion and that had to be maintained. The balance had to be kept, even if Cerberus had tipped it when they'd gone after Harper. I'd heard a few times from Ivar, but only that they were still investigating, still following leads. Nothing tangible to share with Harper. Nothing to keep this event from occurring. While I hated to fucking mingle, I would use this opportunity to get answers that Ivar had yet to uncover. To be face-to-face with Cerberus himself.

"Two hours," I grumbled again. I would look Cerberus

in the eye and learn the truth, to find out if we were now at war. "Two hours and we will be done. You'll meet the leaders of each legion and then we will leave. In the meantime, know that while everyone may be staring at you, they are seeing what they can't have. You belong to me."

"And me," Blade added.

Seeing Harper in a Styx uniform, with the silver band, made me proud. The black didn't hide her curves. She wore it well...when she was wearing it. We hadn't given her much opportunity to do so, keeping her in bed—at least in my quarters—for most of the past week. One of us had been with her at all times. When Blade had left to work on the investigation into the Cerberus fighters who'd attacked Harper, I'd been inside her. Yes, inside. I fucked her and never pulled out when done, sleeping with her on top of me, my cock remaining nice and deep. I wanted the connection —needed it. When I'd had to see to my responsibilities, I knew Blade took very good care of her in and out of bed. While we fucked her together, we would not deny her our cocks if we were apart. Ever.

And now, with everyone looking at us like one would the wild animals on the Hyperion surface, I just wanted to tug her somewhere private and fuck her again. To be away from this bothersome group and alone with our mate.

My cock ached for her, and I didn't give a damn who saw the outline of it my pants.

"Astra," Blade said, tipping his head as way of greeting.

The female leader of the Astra legion stood before us, her uniform identical to ours except for the dark green band on her arm. She was older than I by at least twenty years, although no one knew her exact age and none dared ask. She was shrewd, but not evil. And that put her on the list of people from the other legions I occasionally did business with, even if I never trusted her. Those of us on Rogue 5 knew not to trust very many. Her hair was straight, shorn at her shoulders and a brilliant smoky silver—whether from age or birth I had no idea.

"It is an honor," Astra said, smiling at Harper.

While we had history, and some of it not good, I had to give Astra respect for being courteous enough to approach. Others had not, only stared outright.

"A new planet, two new mates. It must be a drastic change for you." The look on her face, the *smile,* was one I'd never seen before. Coy? Suggestive? I dealt with her as the leader of her legion. She had a keen mind for business and no tolerance for fools. I had seen her hard, relentless, ruthless. Never had I seen her like this. As a woman. A woman with secrets. Perhaps it was because she was speaking with another woman that her demeanor softened.

Harper took a deep breath and gave the legion leader a small smile of her own. "It is, but I have to admit, these two are growing on me."

Astra's smile faltered, but then she laughed. Others turned, curious to learn what was so humorous, but they couldn't hear. "The NPU didn't process what having your mates growing on you means, but I have to assume it is because they are very attentive lovers. By the look of you, you are well satisfied."

Harper's mouth fell open in surprise, and her cheeks turned pink. "That's not—"

"Of course, she is. You doubt our claim, Astra?" I asked, turning the female's attention toward me. While Harper's embarrassment did not seem intentional, she needed a moment.

Astra's gaze shifted to me. "She has yet to be bitten, Styx. You both wear her ink, but she does not carry your bite." She turned her attention back to Harper, her body leaning forward slightly as she took in Harper's scent. "She carries your scent. But I would not wait too long to claim her."

Ah, the legion leader was bold, stating the one thing everyone wanted to know about. Everyone in the room had to be wondering why we had yet to bite our mate. The lack of scars on both sides of her neck was obvious to all. If she'd been from Hyperion, we wouldn't even have asked. Hyperion females didn't want a male to doubt, to hold back. They knew what was to come.

But Harper was human, and the only other human I'd known had blushed with embarrassment at the blatant talk of sex. Of fucking. Of biting and claiming. Earth females required a more delicate touch. Patience. Seduction. Consent.

None of these thoughts and details about Harper were something I would share with a nosy female from another legion, regardless of her rank among our people. She was after one thing. Gossip. I hated gossip.

Blade lifted his free hand, stroked his knuckles over Harper's pink cheeks.

"Perhaps we should resolve that now," he said, looking into our mate's eyes.

They widened, but she remained silent.

"Yes, perhaps we should. Astra." I said her name as a goodbye and followed Blade as he tugged our mate through a side door.

"You seem to keep tugging me into hallways," Harper said, once Blade pushed her up against a wall. We were in a narrow corridor, alone, just like at the canteen on Zenith.

This one, too, led to the outside for emergencies only. No one would come this way.

"We like to have you all to ourselves," Blade replied, running his hands up and down her body as if he couldn't help himself. "We are greedy like that."

"You're not really going to bite me now, are you?" she asked, thrusting her chest out.

Blade cupped her breasts and she sighed. "Is that what you want?" he asked, his voice husky.

We'd fucked her two hours ago, yet we wanted her again. By the way she was squirming and breathing hard, she was just as eager.

"What did we tell you, mate?" I asked, leaning my shoulder against the wall beside them, watching.

"That I'll beg for your bite."

"That's right. But right now, we're going to make you come."

"Again? Now?" Neither word was a protest, and I shared a glance with Blade as we moved into position on either side of her.

"Yes. Do you want to come? Do you want us to touch you, Harper?" I couldn't stop myself. I leaned in and nuzzled her neck with my nose. "Do you want my fingers in your pussy? Stretching you open? Fucking you with them hard and fast?"

She nodded, bit her lip. While she wore the basic uniform as the rest of us, Harper had put her hair up in such a way that it was piled on top of her head. But the pretty style was coming loose as her head slid back and forth against the hard wall. Long tendrils began to fall over her shoulders, and she already looked well-fucked. We couldn't do that here, not now, but we could definitely bring a pretty flush to her cheeks and a softness to her so that everyone in the other room would know that she'd been well-pleased by her mates. That she'd know that we'd take care of her, even with the staring hordes.

"You've got a very greedy pussy," I said, turning her sideways so she leaned her side against the wall, and I stood before her. Blade settled at her back as I undid her pants, loosening them, but not letting them fall.

"Styx," she breathed, putting her hands on my wrists. She looked up at me through her golden lashes, then flicked her gaze toward the door we'd come through. "There are too many people. We're supposed to be at the party."

"Fuck the party," I said, referring to not only fucking, but the sight of her body, the sound of her pleasure. "We want to touch you, and we want to touch you now. Those people will not delay us from being with you, even like this. And we don't share. We want to make you come, mate." I slid my hand over her smooth stomach and watched as she shuddered, melting into me. "I'm greedy, Harper. I want your wet pussy juices coating my fingers. I want to make you lose control, right here, now. Your body is mine, mine to tease, and taste, and fuck."

I slipped a hand down and into her pants, found her dripping and eager, then slid deep inside her wet heat with a firm, quick thrust that had her arching her back, grabbing blindly for my shoulders. Her inner walls clenched as I began to slowly fuck her. It wasn't the same as watching her ride my cock, but it would have to do for now.

I grinned as Blade slowly licked his middle finger, then slid it down the back of her pants. When her eyes flared wide, I covered her mouth with mine, smothering her cry as Blade slipped the single digit into her ass. She loved ass play. Ever since Blade had fucked her there the first day, she wanted it. Craved it. The way her juices practically coated my palm now confirmed it.

"Ride our fingers, mate. Make yourself come," Blade whispered against her neck.

I kept kissing her as she began to undulate her hips back and forth, pressing my finger deeper, then Blade's. She didn't stop, instead picked up her pace as she got closer to her climax.

I lifted my mouth from hers so she could breathe, but I whispered a reminder. "Shh. No one hears you but us."

"Such a naughty girl," Blade murmured, nipping her earlobe. "Getting yourself off while all the leaders of Rogue 5 are just beyond that door."

That did it. Perhaps it was the chance of being caught, or the fact that she loved being double penetrated, or the fact that she was just so fucking responsive, but she came.

She bit her lip and her eyes flared wide, staring at me as she rode out her pleasure.

I grinned at her and my fangs showed. I couldn't hold them back, but would not sink them into her here. Not now. She couldn't miss my need for her even as she milked my finger, wanting more.

As she came back to herself, I praised her. "So beautiful. All ours. Soon it will be our cocks filling you like this. When you beg us to bite you, we'll do it."

"Styx," she breathed. "I want it."

Elation shot through me at her admission. She'd seen my fangs, knew what they looked like, how sharp they were, how they'd have to pierce her tender flesh. Even so, she wanted them. She wanted us.

I wanted to toss her over my shoulder, tell everyone in

the other room to go fuck themselves while we claimed our mate and bit her. But no. We couldn't do that.

I shook my head, brushed her hair back from her face. "Good. When we get you alone, *really alone,* we'll talk about it again."

I slipped from her, brought my glistening finger to my mouth, licked her sweet essence. My mouth watered for more, to drop to my knees and get it right from the source.

I sighed. "First, we must present you to Rogue 5."

"Then, mate, you're ours," Blade agreed, pulling his hand from the back of her pants, reaching around and buttoning her back up.

———

HARPER

THE ALIENS ASSEMBLED IN THE FORMAL ROOM LOOKED ALMOST human.

Almost.

It wasn't the silver hair on multiple heads, like Blade's, that made them look different to those on Earth. It wasn't the too vivid, too bright colors of their eyes that made me shiver as I stood between my mates on the raised platform at the front of the room.

They were *different*. It was in the way they *moved*. The way their eyes focused with absolute, complete attention. Half the time, as someone from one of the various legions approached to greet me, I felt like I was being stared at by a caged tiger, or a mythical shapeshifter, something wild forced to exist in the flesh and blood prison standing before me.

With Styx and Blade, that wildness was intoxicating, sexy. But facing the others, the natural predator in these people, this strange alien race, flooded me with adrenaline as *my* instincts kicked in. The fight or flight response was automatic, and strong. And screaming just one thing...

Run.

But I wasn't an animal, so I told my pounding heart and sweaty palms to shut-up and smiled like I didn't have a care in the world. I knew Styx and Blade would let nothing happen to me. They'd keep me safe even from my wild feelings.

Despite the fact that a member of one of their legions had tried to kill me on Latiri, had ambushed my MedRec team, had leaped onto the transport platform ensuring his own death, none prevented me from doing what I was doing right now. Standing here. On Rogue 5. Alive.

And they were still out there. *Whomever they were.* Styx had said Ivar and some Everian Hunters were looking for the bad guys, but it had been a week. A week of me doing nothing but enjoying the attentions of two very hot, very skilled aliens. No, they weren't aliens here. *I* was the alien. Yet they'd accepted me, even tattooed their skin and pierced their nipples for me. I was slowly weakening when it came to them. No, I was completely theirs. How could I not be? I couldn't count the number of orgasms they'd given me. And the ways they'd done it? Wow.

I was ready for their bite and that scared me. *I was ready to be bitten on the shoulders by two aliens I'd only known for a week while they fucked me at the same time.* Yeah, I was crazy. Crazy in lust. Was I being brainwashed to forget my team?

To forget what had happened to them, what was possibly being done to them all week long while I'd fucked with abandon?

While Ivar and the others were out hunting, I knew Styx had to play politics, had to stand around and chat with the other legions, perhaps learn things about why the group with the red armbands—Cerberus, they'd said—had gone after me. There was more than one way to get answers. This was more hands off than the Hunters searching, but we might learn something. And by the uncomfortable look on Styx's face, I had a feeling it had less to do with the fact that he hadn't come in the hallway than his dislike for parties.

And they'd given me an incredible orgasm. It had helped, a little. I wasn't as nervous. Hell, I was like melted wax, pliable and soft. I just wanted this to be over, but until then, I smiled and nodded as I met them all. Savored the tingles in my girl parts from my mates' eager attentions.

None were allowed to touch me. For that, I was grateful. Not that Styx or Blade would allow it. Only one had even tried, the older woman, the leader named Astra, and she reminded me so much of the overly protective, aggressive helicopter mothers who used to get too much bad press back on Earth, that I held out my hand and shook hers before I thought better of it.

Apparently, it was a big deal, maybe even a political mistake for Styx, because the room went silent when I did it. Maybe shaking hands wasn't a thing on Rogue 5. Maybe it meant something different here like, "I hate you" or something. But Astra looked up from our joined hands into Styx's eyes and nodded at him like some kind of secret was being shared.

Maybe I'd done Styx a favor?

I had no idea. I didn't know these people, didn't know their rules. I didn't know who was friend, who was foe, or who he trusted. Who I was supposed to trust. Which, apparently, was no one. I, at least, knew not to trust those with the red arm bands. I'd probably have nightmares for the rest of my life about the one who'd had a hold of my leg. I felt like a fish out of water—a well taken care of, sexually spoiled, extremely satisfied pet, but still not one of them. I didn't *belong.* I was the alien here, and I felt it in every bone in my body.

"Welcome, legions." Styx cleared his throat and Blade's hand came to rest on the small of my back. The size and heat of his touch were comforting and reminded me of what we'd just done in the back hallway. Styx stood slightly in front of me to protect me from those in the room. They both did that. Protected me. All evening, they'd placed themselves subtly but effectively between me and everyone else. Part of me argued that I should be offended, but I told that old Earth-girl to shut up. We were on an alien moon in a room full of predators. I was very grateful, and more than a little turned on, to have two of the most dangerous males in the room openly declaring their devotion to me. I didn't need to see the ink or the piercings to feel it.

Styx waited for complete silence to linger until I shifted on my feet, uncomfortable as the lack of sound grew heavy and expectant. I recognized the play for what it was, a show of dominance. A demand for respect.

When he was satisfied, he reached back, took my hand, and pulled me up to stand beside him. Blade followed, and I was sandwiched between their muscled frames, each of them pressed to one of my shoulders. "This is our mate, Harper, of Styx legion."

The silence was not broken, and I bit my lip, wondering if I was supposed to say something. Do something. They hadn't needed the verbal introduction. They all knew who I was. It was a proclamation.

Until Astra raised her glass and her enforcers followed suit. Seconds later, every glass in the room was held high as she spoke. "To Harper of Styx."

"Harper of Styx." The room chimed in perfect unison.

Everyone drank. Blade released a breath I hadn't been aware he was holding in a rush of sound, and Styx's shoulders relaxed. He squeezed my hand gently, and I squeezed back. I had no idea what that was all about, but I'd ask them to explain it to me later.

My stomach rumbled, and the scent of fresh fruits and cheeses, some kind of delicious spiced meat almost made me dizzy.

Blade smiled down at me. "Hungry, mate?"

"Starved." I leaned in, whispered, "You gave me quite an appetite."

Styx's arm slid around my waist from behind, and I found myself pressed to his hard heat. No, melting into him was more like it. When it came to these two, I had absolutely zero self-control. It had been all of ten minutes and yet I wanted them again. I knew they were waiting for me to *beg* them to bite me. That the bite was forever. Sacred.

The idea of those two things had scared the shit out of me in the beginning.

Now, I found I wanted them so badly I was afraid to admit it, even to myself. I'd blurted out the request for their bite a short time ago, but they didn't seem to believe me. Or the timing was horrible. Or both. Maybe they thought my arousal had me spouting anything just to come. Maybe it was true.

Maybe being delirious with pleasure simply allowed me to admit a cold, hard truth I couldn't face when I had myself under control.

I wanted them. I wanted what they were offering me. I wanted forever. And that fact scared the hell out of me.

10

SIMPLY PUT, THIS WASN'T GOING TO WORK. I WAS STILL Coalition. My contract not yet fulfilled. Technically, right now, for the entire past week, I'd been A.W.O.L. Missing. That hadn't been brought up because I didn't think Styx and Blade would alter their course. One thing I'd learned on Rogue 5 was that they made their own rules. They didn't follow the Coalition's. In fact, they seemed to all out avoid them. Which meant Styx didn't give a shit that his mate was breaking a whole bunch of Coalition laws. They were considered outlaws and, now, so was I.

Since they didn't seem to worry about pissing off an entire fleet of Interstellar Coalition warriors, I pushed the worry aside. I had bigger problems than being sent to prison for going A.W.O.L. At least I would be alive. My MedRec team might not be so lucky. They were out there somewhere, prisoners or worse. I couldn't forget. I felt helpless trying to solve the mystery of the attack, or helping to bring back my missing crew. I knew nothing of this planet to know where to start a search. I couldn't contact anyone within the Coalition. My hands were tied. I had to rely on others to find them. Styx and Blade assured me the Hunters were searching, that all I had to do was sit back and wait.

Easier said than done. Patience was not my thing. Not when people I cared about were hurting or in danger.

Still, I'd been here, on Rogue 5 getting my mind blown by two skilled, very attentive alien lovers while my team suffered somewhere at the hands of our enemies. I had no choice but to trust in Styx's team, that they would do their job and do it well. If I were to remain here as their mate, it was something I would need to get used to.

In the meantime, Blade leaned in and placed a quick kiss on my lips. I turned from him when an odd sound reached my ears. Like a baseball dropped on hardwood. A thunk. The sound of rolling. I saw the object, metal and round, rolling across the floor. More the size of a softball, but shiny. I followed the path it came from, saw a man staring at me. I sucked in a breath, instantly recognizing him from the Latiri battlefield. Silver hair, pale eyes, empty, indifferent gaze. I'd only seen him for a matter of seconds, but I knew. I would never forget his face. Never.

Something bumped the side of my foot. The softball. When I glanced back up, I saw the grin on his face. Wicked. Menacing.

That was when I heard the beeping. Quiet. So quiet I could barely hear it.

"Styx!" Blade bellowed the warning, kicking the object away from me with the power of a pro-soccer player.

My gaze tore from the familiar face of the stranger, watched Blade's motion. "What—"

Before I could finish my sentence, Styx lifted me and threw both of us to the side, his back to the room, his body curled around mine protectively as the world exploded. I landed hard on my hands and knees, felt Styx's heavy weight against my back.

The boom shattered windows and made my ears ring with pain. Behind me, Styx grunted as the force of the blast hit him in the back.

No one screamed.

Not one fucking person screamed. Shouts came as soon as my hearing returned.

I smelled blood. Not quite human. No heavy metallic tinge of human blood. This was earthier, heavier.

It smelled like death.

I shoved at Styx's hands where they held me to him, but he refused to release me as I heard movement. Scrambling. Orders given in harsh, rough voices by people who were used to fighting. Used to bleeding. Dying.

"Let me go!" I fought him with all my strength, but my muscles were no match for his. I felt the heat of him, the hard lines of his muscles, all taut and tense.

"No." He curled around me even more tightly. I felt his breath on my neck, the hammering of his heart against my back. "Not until Blade gives the all clear."

"Blade could be hurt, you big jerk. Let. Me. Go." I slammed my closed fist into his forearm. Whether he released me or not, there would be no escaping his determination to protect me. "Now. Let me help. If something happens to Blade, I'll never forgive you. Never." It was a low blow; I knew it. But I was shocked to my core to realize it was also true. Blade was mine. He mattered. Not that the others in the room who were injured weren't important, but I spoke the truth. If Blade died because Styx held me back, I'd never forgive him.

Hells bells, I was in love with him. In love with both of these dominant, protective aliens.

Styx's arms loosened, and he rolled away from me. He was on his feet before I'd even turned around. Protecting me. Again.

I stood on shaky legs, ears still ringing, and had to look around Styx's big frame to take in the room. What had happened. There was no fire, only black smoke that rolled toward the ceiling.

Bodies on the floor. Blood. Looks of shock and resignation and pain.

This was a world I knew well. My world for almost two years. Shoving at Styx's shoulder, I pushed past him and yanked a pretty cloth from one of the table decorations. It was clean.

I handed it to Styx, coughed from the smoke. "Tear this into strips, and get me a ReGen wand. Get as many as you can. We're going to need them." I hopped down from the platform and searched for Blade. He groaned, but he was moving. His eyes opened, and he looked up at me from where he was prone on the floor.

"Blade!" I dropped to my knees next to him and ran my hands over every inch of his body with well-practiced efficiency. When he smiled and tried to pull me down for a kiss, I knew he was all right. Styx and Blade were okay.

I could breathe. The world flooded my senses once more, loud and stinking of smoke and chemicals and blood. But I was here. Present. I could think.

Blade reached for me again. "Harper. Harper. Harper." My name was a chant on his lips, and he lifted his head, tried to kiss me.

I pushed him back down, his head bumping the floor with a thump. He grinned.

"I'm not feeling you up, you big oaf. I'm making sure you're not hurt."

He looked down his body, and I followed his gaze, saw the thick outline of his cock beneath his pants. Yeah, he was fine.

Something dark and twisted in my chest loosened and tears gathered on my lashes. I fought them back, kept myself together. I did *not* lose my shit during triage. Period. Instead, I forced myself to grin down at him, tears in my eyes, and leaned over to kiss his cheek. "Don't ever do that again," I ordered. He'd saved me. His David Beckham kick had sent the bomb away from the center of the room, away from most of the people in attendance.

"I will do whatever I have to, Harper, to keep you safe."

That proclamation earned him another teary kiss, but I had to move on. My nursing instincts were screaming at me to get moving. People were going to bleed out. Die.

I nodded in response, then turned from him, scanning the room. "Others need my help."

Without waiting for him to respond—since he might decide to keep me from helping—I went to the nearest legion member not moving. Yellow. Blue. Green. Red. Silver. I ignored the arm bands as I triaged, assessing wounds. Right now I didn't care what political bullshit this moon base had going on. People were hurt.

Blade struggled to his feet as Styx followed me, handed me makeshift bandages from the cloth I'd given him, dutifully tearing it into pieces for me. When a ReGen wand appeared at my shoulder, I reached for it and smiled my thanks up at my beautiful, powerful mate. He never left my side. He assisted me in my tasks, but didn't hinder.

Even when I came to *him.* I gasped. "You," I breathed.

He was conscious, sweating, his face devoid of color. The reason was obvious. Blood spurted from a large cut in his thigh, high. Thank god the blood wasn't spurting with every heartbeat, but the amount of blood seeping through his fingers was telling. If I'd had to guess, I'd say his femoral vessel had been cut. And while his hands covered it, tried to tamp the flow, that wasn't going to stop him from bleeding out in the next couple minutes.

"Do you know this Kronos male?" Blade asked from my opposite side.

I ignored his question. It was irrelevant to my patient's survival. "Give me a strip of cloth or a belt. Now, or he'll die."

The Kronos male I was treating had just tried to hurt me, hurt a lot of people with that explosion, but I was in nursing mode now.

All life mattered. Even his. What he'd done didn't matter in this instance.

I had no idea who held a strap from an ion rifle over my shoulder, but it wasn't Styx. I didn't care if magical fairies delivered it. I grabbed it, nudged the dying man's hands out of the way, tucked it around his thigh and tugged. Made a tie, then tugged again.

"Grab this side," I told Blade with a calm, commanding voice when he knelt beside me, holding out one end of the strap for him to take.

He gripped it and I pulled, cinching the band tighter

and tighter until the bleeding slowed to a trickle and I could knot if off, making a tourniquet.

"This wound is too severe for a wand. He needs a ReGen Pod. Tell the doctor to repair that vein before he removes the tourniquet. If he doesn't get medical attention now, he's going to lose that leg."

Two big guys picked him up, one beneath the arms, the other at his ankles and carried him from the room. As I moved to stand, Blade stopped me with a hand on my biceps.

"You recognized him. Why?"

Our hands were bloody, Blade's face covered in soot. I could only imagine I looked just as bad. The injured were being carried away or treated where they were with ReGen wands. I saw the female leader, Astra, tending to someone with a small cut to the forehead. I could take a moment and clear my head, slow my breathing and listen. The smoke had cleared, but the scent of charred wood and a burning that reminded me oddly of fireworks from the Fourth of July still filled the air. I was sweating beneath the black uniform.

I saw the narrowing of Blade's eyes. The heightened awareness as he waited for me to respond. Not only did he want an answer, but he was on alert for any new danger. Perhaps that was why I could subconsciously take a breath because I knew he would keep me safe. He'd done it with the softball shaped bomb, and I knew he could do it again.

"Yes." I took a deep breath, let it out. All the good endorphins from the hallway orgasm were gone. Now I was coming down from an adrenaline high. "From the ambush on Latiri. I recognized him. He was one of them. One of the men from the shuttles."

Blade frowned. "I didn't know there were any Kronos in the battle."

"Those with yellow arm bands? There weren't," I countered.

Blade stood abruptly, tugged me up with him. "Styx!" he shouted.

Within a second, Styx appeared, looked me over, ran his hands down my arms, then took my hands, flipped them over so the sticky, stained palms were up. "You are injured?"

"The blood's not hers," Blade clarified, as if he could read his leader's thoughts.

When Styx loosened his hold, I wiped my hands on my pants, not realizing until he'd looked how stained they were.

"The Kronos with the leg wound," Blade said. "He was at Latiri with Harper."

Styx stiffened, eyed me. I could practically see his mind working.

"Come."

Styx led the way out of the room, moving around people, all either well or on their way to it. I could see my services weren't needed, and I doubted either Styx or Blade would allow me to remain here without them nearby to protect me after my news.

"Where are we going?" I asked, trying to keep pace with his quick gait.

"To the med unit to question the Kronos about Latiri," Styx said.

"He's the one who tossed the bomb," I said, dropping a bomb of my own.

That got Styx to freeze, and I almost bumped into his back. He spun about, looked down at me, put his hands on my shoulders. "You saw him do it?"

Obviously, he hadn't.

I nodded. "Yes, but I don't understand. Those on Latiri who I saw, the group who came in the two shuttles, the one who came through the transport with me, all had red armbands." I pointed down the hallway in the direction of the med unit. "He had a yellow one."

"Kronos," Blade clarified. He looked thoughtful for a moment. "Red indicates Cerberus. You're sure—"

"You *killed* the one who grabbed me just before transport. You saw his armband. It was red." I wondered how he could question that when he'd snapped the guy's neck. "Why are the Kronos and Cerberus legions after me? What have I done?"

I was just a MedRec team member from Earth. No one exciting. I did my job, got in and out. Nothing more. Why would they be after me?

Styx spun about and continued walking. He was halfway down the hallway before he spoke again. "You saw them at Latiri. You're a witness," he called from over his shoulder. I'd never seen him walk so fast before.

I ran to keep up, Blade on my heels. "To what?" I asked, my breath coming quickly.

"To the attack on Latiri. You saw their faces." Even when he was getting my name tattooed on his skin I hadn't seen the same intensity in his gaze as I did now.

"What are you going to do?" I asked, concerned. "The Kronos or Cerberus guy—or whatever legion he's from—is in no shape to answer questions."

The door to the med unit slid open. Within, it was busy, the most critical of patients from the explosion were being tended.

"Interrogate him," Styx said, his voice deep. His eyes

hard. He turned to enter, but I grabbed his arm. He looked over his shoulder at me.

"Now? You can't. He'll die."

Styx didn't respond, instead walked in and went down the line of ReGen Pods until he found the one he was looking for.

"Styx!" I cried. The male was awake, but barely. His eyes were open, but vacant; I doubted he even noticed we were there. The tourniquet was still applied as the pod was being readied. A doctor was waving a wand over the wound as someone else moved an injector toward his neck.

"Not yet," Styx said, stalling the male's action.

I grabbed Styx, but he was immovable. "I did my job and saved him."

He looked down at me, his green eyes piercing. "And now it is my turn to do my job as leader of this legion and get answers. I need him conscious."

"Wait until he is well," I countered. The male had lost too much blood to be able to answer any kind of question, even his name.

"Why?" he asked, through clenched teeth. "I'll only hurt him all over again."

This was a different side of Styx I'd never seen before. I knew the moon base was ruthless, the people lawless. Without the presence of the Coalition, the legions ruled with a "take matters into your own hands" mentality.

Was he really planning to hurt, or worse kill, this injured man once he had the information he needed?

"Styx." I said his name, but either he was ignoring me or didn't care about my concerns. I spun on my heel, put my hand on Blade's chest. "What's going to happen?" I asked him.

Blade lifted a hand to stroke over my hair, but when he saw the blood—this man's blood—he dropped it. "He would have killed you or taken you with your MedRec team from the Latiri battlefield. And now he's tossed an ion cannon at you, at us. We must know the reason why."

"Even if it kills him?" I asked.

Blade nodded. "His life was over the moment he tried to hurt you."

I turned to Styx, prepared to argue, but the unforgiving slant of his jaw was chilling, and I knew there would be no debate, no mercy for the man I'd just tried so hard to save.

I walked to Styx and stood in front of him, blocking his way as the doctor and one of the others lifted the man into a ReGen Pod and removed the tourniquet from his leg. Styx stiffened, but I pressed my forehead to his chest and wrapped my arms around him. "He's not going to give you answers if he's dead."

I felt more than saw Styx nod at the doctor to allow him to start the healing cycle in the pod. Perhaps I'd done the man an injustice, perhaps it would have been better to let him die. I could only imagine what Styx would do to him. He was so possessive of me, just as protective as Blade, but he also had to see justice done. As leader, he couldn't let one of his own down.

Even as I thought it, my mind rebelled. We needed answers. We had one of the attackers in our grasp, someone who would know where my team had been taken. Someone who knew the identity of the traitor on Zenith. Someone who could tell us everything.

Even if Blade and Styx had to torture him, beat him, ravage him for the information?

I thought of my team, of the dead on the battlefield, of

the brave Atlan, Warlord Wulf, who'd nearly bled to death to save me, and my anger grew until I could live with the choice being made. It made me sick, but I couldn't see any other solution.

Condemning that man to death, knowing what would happen once he woke, broke something inside me, something I'd never thought could be broken, but I knew Styx was right.

We needed him alive. We needed him to talk.

And after?

I wouldn't think about after.

Maybe I was an animal after all.

11

S tyx

MY ENFORCERS CIRCLED THE ROOM LIKE HUNGRY RAPTORS waiting for the communication link to be established. The Kronos soldier had been taken from the ReGen Pod, taken one look at my face, and begged for a quick end. He should.

My soft-hearted mate argued to spare his life, tried to convince me he deserved to live. But he'd killed countless members of her team on Latiri, taken more hostage, and tried to kill the one person in the galaxy whose life I placed above all others.

Hers.

Harper may have wanted me to spare him, but the Kronos was a dead man, and he knew it.

He'd told us everything, and, as promised, I'd allowed Cormac to take him away and end things quickly. Painlessly.

The bastard didn't deserve such mercy, but it would

make my mate happy, so I contented myself with knowing he was dead, that we had some answers.

Silver and Blade stood together, talking quietly where they leaned against the wall. The siblings were close, their connection apparent since the moment of their birth. They'd come into the world together, fought together. Perhaps one day they would die together. Twins were rare among our kind, and these two were a bit of a legend.

Khon twirled his dagger on the table, the rhythmic noise unnerving. But I ignored the impulse to snarl at him to stop. When Cormac walked in, Blade, Harper and I all looked up at once. He looked only at me, the slight nod of his head all the confirmation I needed that the traitor was dead.

Harper bit her lip and blinked, hard, but she didn't protest. Not again. She'd fought hard for him, saving his life, until I reminded her that he'd been responsible for the deaths of countless members of her MedRec team, and probably many more. Even in the Coalition there were rules about traitors, about the guilty. What we did with him was nothing new for her. While she had a healing spirit and it went against her nature, she had to know—better than others—that he was guilty and faced the consequences of his callous actions.

She still didn't like it, but she rose from her seat and crossed the room. To me. For comfort. Solace.

I wrapped my arms around her and held her close, inhaled her scent into my lungs. Now that the traitor was dead and I knew who was behind the recent string of attacks on the Coalition, something loosened in my chest. Not only for Harper, but for the entire population of Rogue 5.

We were not part of the Coalition, but we existed in their space. And the foolish act of taking live prisoners, of attacking their medical teams, was tantamount to suicide for all the legions, not just Styx. Without the truth, the Coalition could invade, destroy us.

The Prime on Prillon was not known for his mercy. Prime Nial and his second, a brutish warrior named Ander, ruled with iron control. They were fair, but they were hard, hard warriors. Not pampered royal asses like their predecessors. When I learned that their mate was also a female from Earth, I suspected she was often one of the only things that held them in check.

If I didn't get the attacks on Coalition personnel under control, they would rain down fire on my moon, on my people. I was a pirate and a rebel. We had neither the ships nor the manpower to take on the Fleet.

"Styx." The voice coming through the comm screen was harsh, direct. Doctor Mersan of the Intelligence Core didn't mince words. A fact I appreciated because I wasn't in the mood. My mate was safe, but my world was in peril.

"Mersan."

Harper tried to pull free from my arms, but I held her to me. I did allow her to turn around and face the Coalition officer who would decide her fate. And his.

"Doctor Mersan?" Harper's questioning voice brought a smile to the crafty bastard's face. Apparently, he liked my mate. I bit back a growl of possessiveness. He was a light year away, but I didn't trust him. Not with what was important to me. But it was time to make a deal, and I needed him for it.

"What's the emergency, Styx? This better be good." What he didn't say was that by contacting him directly like this, Blade and I risked our association with the Coalition's intelligence network might be revealed. We might be rogue, but some parts of the Coalition liked us for it. Used it to their advantage.

But my people lived in the darkness. I knew how to get around their surveillance systems, their trackers and lies. "I've got information on the MedRec team taken in the Latiri system. I know where they're holding the prisoners, the weapons." I grinned now, pausing to make sure the good doctor was listening, and by the way he sat up straight in his chair and leaned forward, he was. "And the mobile transport tags."

His eyes narrowed, but he focused on Harper's face. "Ms. Harper Barrett from Earth. You were listed among the missing on the Latiri report."

She stiffened, but didn't try to pull away from me again. "Warlord Wulf saved me. Then Styx and Blade brought me to Rogue 5."

"I can see that." His gaze tracked over my possessive hold, the way Harper relaxed into my arms. He didn't need to be a doctor to know the way things were. "What do you want, Styx?"

"I want Harper's record cleared. I want her out of the Fleet, free and clear. She's mine."

His gaze narrowed further until he looked cruel. Annoyed. But Harper held her ground, and my enforcers sat quietly, watching the exchange. "Is this what you want, Harper?"

She took a deep breath, and I saw her gaze lock with Blade's, his victorious grin. "Yes. I want to stay here. On Rogue 5."

The Prillon's smile through the vid screen was not amused. He eyed her for a moment, then looked to me, all but dismissing Harper. "I will trade your mate's freedom for information, Styx. I want everything."

It was my turn to smile. Yes, he was predictable, just as I'd suspected. Harper was just a MedRec team member who was almost finished with her two-year volunteer service. One of many. Hundreds. Thousands. To him, the trade wasn't even. He thought he was getting more. He was wrong.

I could tell him the truth, give him the information freely and in its entirety and get him to do the dirty work for me. All while I was fucking and claiming my mate, a resource he tossed aside.

"I had no doubt," I replied. "But I have one condition."

"And what might that be?"

"Styx legion will be on the mission. These are my enemies, Mersan. And they tried to kill my mate. I want blood." I held his gaze, warrior to warrior so he'd understand the full extent of my rage. Harper was mine; Rogue 5 was mine. And these traitors had almost destroyed everything. I would give them to Mersan, but I'd see them finished.

"Done. I'll send transport coordinates." The screen went blank less than a second later, and Harper spun to face me.

"No," she said, her voice full of fear. Her eyes held the same. "You can't go. Let them take care of it."

Cormac answered for me. "The traitors are ours, too, Harper. Their blood is ours."

She glanced from warrior to warrior, lingering on Silver, one woman to another. But my mate underestimated the bloodlust and demands of honor among my people. Silver was female, and perhaps on Earth they were considered the lesser gender, but on Rogue 5, her blood ran even hotter than the rest.

"I'm going to make them bleed, Harper," Silver told her. "I'm going to kill them slowly. Their actions threatened my family. Could bring down the Coalition on us. Do you understand the extent of what they could do? Without them finished—and knowing it's done—we will always be looking over our shoulders. Worried. With this deal, the Coalition sees us as being helpful, courteous even."

That word, *courteous,* was almost distasteful to hear. That wasn't us.

"As for the traitors, I will take pleasure in killing them." She all but cracked her knuckles in eagerness to see this done.

Harper's shoulders slumped, and I lifted my hands to massage the tense muscles. "They are evil, Harper. They broke our laws as well as those of your Coalition. They must be dealt with."

"Fine." She leaned her head back against my shoulder and sighed. "But I don't want the gory details. I really don't."

Blade crossed the small room and stroked her cheek with gentle fingers. He was as ready as the rest of us to see this done. "Never, mate. We protect you in all things."

Khon looked up from a tablet screen and put his blade away. "Mersan came through. Coordinates received, Styx."

Mersan hadn't wasted a second. He wanted to see this done as much as we did. No, he wanted the information. Immediately.

Cormac tilted his head from side to side, cracking his neck with a loud snap. "Let's go."

Blade leaned down and kissed Harper, hard and fast. "I will see you soon, mate."

The others bowed slightly to both of us as they followed him out of the room.

I turned Harper in my arms and took her mouth slowly, gently, determined to savor her.

Her hands fisted in my uniform, and she was trembling. "You better come back to me. You and Blade promised."

I tucked her hair behind her ear. "And which promise are you referring to, mate?"

"Bite me, Styx. I want you both to be mine."

"We are already yours."

"Forever, Styx. I want forever. I want that bite, and you're going to give it to me."

"Bossy. I like it." I grinned—showing her my fangs that appeared because of her tone—kissed her once more, then was gone.

———

BLADE

LEAVING HARPER WAS THE HARDEST THING I'D EVER HAD TO do. The brush of her lips on mine wasn't enough. She'd said she was ready to be claimed, ready for us to bite her, and yet we had to go track down traitors. I'd never cared before about cleaning up scum. It's what we did. But now? Now I had more. Now I had Harper.

I knew she was safe.

We tasked Scribe and Ivar with protecting her while we were gone and they'd do so with their lives. Neither Styx nor I could sit out this fight. The need for blood was like a fever inside me. These traitors had attacked Harper, tried to kill our mate. Orchestrated an attack at our mating feast.

They were dead. Every fucking one of them was dead. I wouldn't be able to sleep at night until this was done.

Blood for blood.

They went after Harper. They would die.

The coordinates were programmed in, and within seconds of stepping on the transport pad, we were with Mersan. He stood next to Styx at the front of the bay talking to our enforcers and his Coalition warriors. There were close to a hundred killing machines listening. These weren't standard Coalition warriors. These were Intelligence Core. Killers, spies. A good number of Everian Hunters stood among us and more than two dozen Atlan beasts. The rest were Prillon warriors, hunting in pairs.

I'd never considered my people small. Weak.

But in this room of elite killers, we'd barely be able to hold our own.

For once, I was fine with that. I was fine to be considered *less*. If Mersan thought that and used his very large, very skilled resources to root out the fuckers, then I was fine with that. Whatever needed to happen to keep the Coalition away from Rogue 5 and us in bed with Harper as soon as possible.

Styx stood next to the doctor, arms crossed, a fierce scowl on his face. He looked exactly like what he was—a brutal, merciless killer. A king among outlaws. As I watched several of the Coalition warriors watch him with nervous glances, I was proud. Pride that these big, huge fuckers were wary of my leader made me want to grin. But I stifled it. Stifled everything but my need to kill.

Fuck the Coalition. Fuck the Atlans and the Prillons and the Everian Hunters. We were here for *our* people. For our mate. And Doctor Mersan didn't want anyone in the

Coalition to know he was on to the smuggling ring. Which was why every killer in the room wore black and silver. Styx colors.

It was the only time Styx would allow such a thing. Only those honorable enough wore our colors, but this time, this *one* time, we'd follow Mersan's plan and everyone would appear to be part of the legion.

Styx was using the Coalition to send a message to Kronos they wouldn't soon forget. All the legions would hear the news, about the monsters about to descend on their cargo ship and wreak havoc. Styx's legend would grow. No one would fuck with us, or our mate. Not the Coalition, not Kronos or any other legion thinking of fucking with us.

With the fury building in me, the others would have to get in line if they wanted vengeance of their own. I'd see mine done first. For Harper.

"I want the leadership alive," Doctor Mersan announced to the warriors, but Styx's response was immediate.

"Then you'd better get to them first."

A couple of the Atlans chuckled at Styx's quiet proclamation, but everyone in the room knew he was completely serious. There would be no mercy from him. From the Styx legion. I moved to stand beside Styx, shoulder to shoulder. There would be no mercy from me either. Not when they'd attacked what was mine.

Beside me, Cormac's grin nearly split his face. His hunger, his need to protect his people, his leader, his family, was even more primitive and instinctive than most. The rage emanating from him fed my own until it took everything I had to wait. To listen. I had no idea how he managed to control himself.

"Wager?" Khon spoke from Cormac's right, keeping his voice tipped low.

Silver leaned around me and the huge warrior and shook her head at Khon. "Bet against Styx and you'll lose."

Khon smiled, slapped me on the shoulder. "My money's not on Cormac, it's on Blade."

Silver laughed at that. "How can I bet against my own brother?"

I didn't look at either of them, instead stared out at the group of warriors who would have our backs, then at our leader. "You'll lose."

Silver punched me on the other shoulder. "Fifty on Styx."

"Done." Khon held out his hand and they shook on it as Mersan and Styx led the way to the transport pads.

I stepped in behind, my heart rate kicking up, my senses sharpening. Time to hunt.

12

THE MOMENT THE TWISTING PAIN OF TRANSPORT LOOSENED ITS grip on me, I spun, blades out. Ready. I had no intention of using ion blasters. I wanted my enemies to look into my eyes when I gutted them.

The cargo ship was large for a vessel of this type. And the traitor told us to expect a crew of close to fifty with twice that many prisoners and several bays full of stolen weapons, medical supplies, and almost a thousand mobile transport tags used by the medical teams to evacuate the wounded.

They were worth more on the black market than everything else combined—including the ship itself.

Apparently, Kronos legion had been busy raiding, stealing, looting. Harper's team was one of many that had been attacked. The Intelligence Core wanted some of them alive. I grimaced at that, the word *some*. They didn't give a fuck about them. They were commodities, and it was a good thing Harper was safe on Rogue 5 or Mersan would be a dead man along with the traitor for his indifference. But in this moment, I needed that indifference to get what I wanted. Mersan was looking for the traitor on their side of this mess, the medical officer feeding Kronos the locations and other information on the MedRec teams when they went out into the field.

I didn't care about what Mersan wanted. He could find that traitor and lead me directly to Kronos.

That legion needed to go down. I wanted blood.

Mersan split his men into teams with a wave of his hand, and a group of Prillon and Atlan warriors moved quickly in the direction of the prisoner holding cells. Fortunately, we were not only given the location of the ship, but the blueprints for them as well. We'd studied them, knew where to go.

His second team moved to attack the cargo areas and recover the weapons and other goods stored there.

A third team would head for the command deck and take over the ship, capture their leaders.

They moved quickly, silently. Efficiently. But not fast enough.

Blade ran beside me, Cormac, Silver and Khon right behind us as we moved so quickly I knew we were barely more than a blur. Only the Everian Hunters could outrun us, and they'd been sent to the prison block at my insistence. They could get there with their intense speed and save the innocent.

The sounds of battle and ion blasts echoed through the corridors. The ship's alert system went to flashing red. Beside me, Blade growled. "They know we're coming."

They'd known the second our group touched down on the transport pad.

The smile that stretched my face was feral. "Good."

Behind us, the pounding boots of at least two dozen Coalition warriors thundered down the narrow walkway, but they were nearly a minute behind us.

Everyone on the command deck would be dead before they arrived.

Kronos had betrayed not just Styx legion, but all Hyperions on Rogue 5 when they pulled their raids. They threatened our existence. If the Coalition Fleet decided to wage war on us, one battleship would be all it would take to turn our moon base into a crater in seconds.

We were smugglers, pirates. We didn't draw attention to ourselves, and we didn't bring down hell itself with uncontrolled greed.

The Fleet ignored us because we made it easy for them to do so. We operated, we kept the peace, we kept the black market under control. Every once in a while, tossed them a bone and offered assistance. Like now, although this time, we only let them think they were in charge.

But if we slipped the leash, pulled too hard, men like Mersan would destroy everything our people had built. Our truce was uneasy, balanced on a razor's edge. And Kronos had fucked with the system. Gotten greedy. Tried to take too much. To take people. We didn't do slaves.

Astra, Cerberus and Siren had all agreed with my plan when I contacted them to let them know my intended course of action. I hadn't asked their permission to kill the bastards either. Luckily, the others had been in agreement. Every Kronos legionnaire on this ship would die today.

We met little resistance as we rushed down the hall. Two

guards stood at the entrance to the command deck, their bodies blocking the large doors, their arm bands telltale yellow. Not red.

They were not hiding who they were here. Either they were cocky fuckers who didn't care or they never imagined we'd find them and bring them down. That cockiness was at the core of every Hyperion, but today, it would destroy them.

They didn't flinch as they fired at us in a steady stream, their blasters set on the highest setting.

The first shot hit me in the shoulder, but I barely felt the sting. Our bodies were different than the other races in the Coalition. Our armor custom made to distribute ionic charges—something Mersan knew nothing about. I wasn't injured like a fighter would have been. No, I was enraged. The strike only grew my need to kill.

I rushed the guard on the left as Blade ran toward his companion.

A killing rage was upon me as I wondered if this man had laid his hands on my mate. Had shot that ion blaster at her on Latiri.

Blade's bellow echoed down the corridor like a cannon blast as he shoved his guard up against the door and buried a blade in his throat. The strike was ruthless, the death swift, but it no doubt helped his blood lust.

I was feeling less civilized, but more in control. I wanted to kill the guard before me, yes, but I also wanted to send a message.

Holding the Kronos soldier up against the wall by his neck, I looked over my shoulder at Silver. "Record this. I want it played on every comm on Rogue 5."

Her grin was pure evil as she adjusted a sensor on her uniform and nodded.

Looking into the recording device, I narrowed my eyes and held the Kronos soldier still, my grip sure. His hands wrapped around mine, tugging, fighting for air. I ignored him and addressed my people.

"I am Styx. This soldier from Kronos is part of an operation that attacked the Coalition MedRec teams. Not only did Kronos disobey Legion Law in attacking outright, endangering all of us with their reckless taunting of the Coalition Fleet, he attacked my mate."

Blade stepped next to me, his gaze fixed on the man I still held pinned to the wall. Face sprayed with blood, hands coated with it, he turned and faced the camera, fangs on display as he snarled his own version of a warning to anyone who might be watching.

"This is what happens to my enemies." Turning, I ripped the offender's throat from his neck with one hand and dropped his body to the ground with the loosening of my fingers. The scent of blood and death filled the air, filled my nostrils, making my fangs drop, too. Dangling the remains of his breathing tube and bloody flesh in my hand, I turned back to the camera and spoke in the calmest, coldest voice I could manage. "This is not Styx legion in a rage. This is not Styx losing control. This," I dangled the bloody mess one more time before lowering it and taking a step closer to the camera. "This is what I do to my enemies. This is what I do to those who harm my mate. The rules about mates is bigger than Coalition Law. Than Legion Law. No planet, no leader in the universe will deny the need for revenge against those who would harm a mate. Let it be known what they have done and how I will finish them."

"Send that to Rogue 5 now," I said. "Right fucking now. We should play it morning, noon and night on every broadcast channel."

I wanted the truth known. Unrest to end. The betrayers to cease to exist.

The Coalition fighters caught up to us in the hall. Their leader, a huge Prillon warrior with dark skin and amber eyes, frowned when he saw the carnage. "We were to take them alive, Styx."

"They went after our mate," I said, telling him what he missed because of their slow approach.

Apparently, that was enough explanation, because the Prillon dismissed the bodies with barely a flicker of his eyes as he pointed his ion blaster toward the door. I had to wonder if he had a mate and a second back on Prillon Prime. "Let's end this," he said. Duty and honor were both reasons for him to complete his mission.

Blade looked at me. No question, we were going in first. "Ready?"

I nodded, and he lifted the dead guard's hand to press it to the door scanner, blood smearing as he did so.

The door slid open and we rushed inside, ready to fight. Ready to kill.

But Mersan was already there. The entire Kronos command crew was on their knees, their hands and feet locked in metallic restraints so strong even an Atlan in beast mode couldn't break them.

The doctor stood over the highest-ranking enforcer from Kronos, a man Blade and I had known for years.

"What are you doing here, Mersan? These men are mine."

Doctor Mersan tapped the mobile transport beacon stuck to his chest. "You're too slow, Styx. They're mine now."

"Are you trying to play me for a fool?" I took two steps forward, ready to rip his head from his shoulders, but the Prillon at my back raised their weapons. I wouldn't make it. They'd won.

"Stand down, Styx," Mersan ordered, not looking at me.

I knew he was right, knew I needed to let him do his job, track the rest of the traitors, discover what their plans were, if they had other cargo ships. Other contacts. More informants scattered throughout the Coalition Fleet.

But that was Mersan's problem. Not mine.

"You can have the rest, Mersan." I pointed to the Kronos leader. "He's mine."

The doctor shook his head. "I need him alive."

I glanced around the room, at the eight additional captives Mersan had taken. None enforcers in Kronos, but all Hyperion people I recognized. "You have more than enough prisoners."

"Gods be damned, Styx, he's mine."

Mersan was an ally. He was the only contact I had powerful enough to make sure Harper was removed from the Coalition Fleet's claws. They owned her. I'd break the law, fight a war to keep her. But that would make my people bleed. Better to sacrifice this one kill. For Harper. For all the people of Rogue 5. For my legion. "Get him out of my fucking sight."

Mersan nodded at the other Coalition warriors around the room and they affixed mobile transport tags to their prisoners. One by one, they disappeared into thin air as we watched. They would go to a Coalition prison. Stand trial, ultimately be executed for their actions. They *would* die, but I was denied the blood we wanted. Denied our vengeance.

I met and held Mersan's gaze. "Promise me he will suffer."

The curl of Mersan's lips was cruel. He was supposed to be a healer, like Harper. But his heart was as black as hers was light. In this moment, I was glad. He knew my need, shared it to a certain degree.

"You have my word, Styx."

Blade's chest heaved beside me, his hands clenching into fists at his sides as the prisoners around us disappeared, until only the enforcer was left.

The bastard raised his eyes to mine, looked behind me at Blade, Silver, and the others, his gaze flickering as he took inventory of the enforcers who had come to end him. He grinned at Blade, his fangs showing.

"How's your pretty little mate? She's quick on her feet. I missed her three times before that Atlan bastard started firing back." He tilted his head to the side, as if pondering a philosophical question during a grandmother's dinner party. "Tell me, did you bite her when you took her ass? Or did you save her for me?"

Blade moved so fast even I didn't see him.

"No!" I yelled, the one word echoing off the walls.

Mersan didn't get the chance to protest, his Prillon reflexes too slow for Blade's rage.

Blade's hands wrapped around the enforcer's neck and he twisted. Hard. Fast. Too hard.

He bellowed when the bones snapped, cracked. Kept twisting, rage on his face and in his eyes. There was no thinking man beneath the instincts raging at him.

I realized, as the enforcer's head was detached from his

body, that he was smiling. He'd taunted Blade, known his protective rage would save him weeks or months of torture at Mersan's hands. He knew he would die and chose his own ending. Chose to fuck with Blade and get exactly what he wanted. Instant death.

Mersan snarled at him, but I moved quickly, stepping between Blade and the Prillon spy. If Blade hadn't done it, I would have. "You have other prisoners, Mersan."

"He was their leader," he shouted, raising his arm in the direction of the headless Kronos. Blade could end up in jail himself for what he'd just done, gone against orders.

"No," I countered. "He was a Kronos enforcer."

The Prillon took a moment to calm himself as Blade threw the detached head against the wall with a bellow. The sound of flesh striking metal was thick and heavy, sloppy and wet. Blood streaked down the wall, began to pool on the floor. The scent of it was strong, cloying.

The sound was extremely satisfying. I smiled as Blade walked back to us, covered in blood from the enforcer and the guard he'd ended in the corridor outside. He'd gotten the revenge he wanted. I had gotten mine, although by Blade's hands. That was good enough for me.

"By the gods, let's get out of here, Mersan." The Prillon commander who'd followed us into the room from the hall spoke now. "The charges are set. The prisoners evacuated. All the cargo has been off-loaded and transported out."

"Gods damned fucking Hyperions." Mersan cursed us, but we didn't bother to respond. I didn't give a fuck what he thought.

Mersan looked down at the headless corpse and sighed. "Were the ship's records downloaded for analysis?"

"Yes, sir."

"Fine." Mersan spoke to the Prillon, but he looked at me. "Get the fuck off this ship. I don't want to see you again."

I dipped my chin slightly in acknowledgement. "The feeling, Prillon, is mutual." We both knew it was impossible. Blade and I were their contact to the black market, the pirates, the criminal elements in Coalition space. He needed us, and we needed him.

Didn't mean we liked each other.

Mersan slapped a transport tag on his chest and disappeared, leaving the dead behind to burn with the ship. And if we didn't transport out, we'd burn with it. Like Mersan cared. Our safety was not his problem.

Behind me, Cormac cleared his throat. "I win, Silver. Pay up."

"Bastard." Her voice was full of laughter, and she grumbled as we followed the Coalition team back to the transport pads. "Too many fucking aliens. Didn't save any bad guys for me."

Khon looked back over his shoulder. "If you want to choke something, Silver, my cock is willing and available. And hard, after this."

"Shut up, Khon."

Blade fell into step beside me, and we lagged back a few paces. "I couldn't do it, Styx. I couldn't let him live. Not after all that had happened, and especially after what he said."

I grabbed his shoulder and squeezed my thanks. "I couldn't kill him. It was too big a risk. But since we share a mate, I am glad it was you who claimed Harper's vengeance. Your hands or mine, the deed is done."

The fucker was dead, no matter who'd ripped his head from his shoulders.

Our gazes locked and he understood. Harper was ours.

Every cell in my body demanded that asshole's death. By my hand or Blade's made no difference to me. But by Blade doing it, Mersan couldn't blame me. The political ramifications were kept to a minimum. We'd offer our services to the Fleet someday in the future, but not before Mersan took time to cool off. We'd gotten what we wanted. Revenge. Our mate.

The ship was set to detonate; there was no more time to talk. We walked into the transport room, the others waiting on the pad.

"Let's go home and finish what we started," I told him, all at once ready to be back with Harper. The mission was complete. We had something else to focus on now. And how sweet it would be. My balls ached and my fangs dropped remembering how good her pussy tasted, how tight she was. How much tighter she'd be when she took both our cocks at the same time. As we bit her.

Blade smiled, his fangs still out. He shifted his cock in his pants as the pull of the transport made the hair on my arms rise.

Time to take what was ours.

Time to bite Harper and claim her forever.

13

*H*arper

THEY WERE HERE. THEY WERE WHOLE.

Styx came through the door first, Blade directly behind. Styx's green gaze met mine, held as he stalked toward me.

When I first met him on Zenith, when he'd approached me at the bar, he'd had the same intensity, as if there was no one else in the universe but me. It was unnerving then.

Now? Now, I wanted that unwavering attention. I wanted everything he could give me. Attention. Love. Obsession.

Maybe it was wrong or stupid or a hundred other things I didn't want to think about or try to analyze, but for the first time in my life, I felt like someone *saw me*. I'd never really been alone in my life, surrounded by people who worked hard and fought as hard as I did. It took meeting Styx and Blade to realized I hadn't been alone—but I'd been lonely.

I went around the control panel, all but knocking Ivar

down and launched myself into Styx's hold. He was all hard, lean muscle. Heat. Power. I felt it as one arm banded about my back, the other beneath my butt. I melted into him as if we were two pieces of a jigsaw puzzle clicking into place. I breathed him in. Closed my eyes and let his heat soothe all the jagged edges, the hours of agitation and worry and terror that they'd be hurt, not come back to me.

His breath fanned my neck as he breathed me in, and I felt the brush of his lips, the flick of his tongue and even the graze of his teeth. I whimpered at the feel. Innocent, but the meaning was clear. He would bite me. Soon. The promise in that light touch made my heart leap and tears fill my eyes. I wanted him. Wanted them. Forever.

"Mate," he growled.

"Mine," I replied.

I pulled my head back enough to look into his eyes, then over his shoulder at Blade. I reached out my hand, and he took it, felt his strength, too.

Needed it. It was as if I'd lost the connection, their energy, when they left Rogue 5. But now, god, I was addicted and didn't want to live without this feeling, without them, ever again. Every minute they were away was agony. I'd been restless, nauseated. Panicked, even. Scribe and Ivar had done their best to reassure me, to tell me of their fighting prowess. They'd even gone so far as to say my mates' blood lust, their need for revenge would protect them.

I saw it as blinders, potentially putting them in harm's way. But I'd been wrong. Thank god.

"Are you hurt?" I asked, looking them both over as best I could. I didn't see any blood, no dirt or torn clothes. It didn't even appear they'd been in battle at all. Not any battle I was used to.

I felt Styx's chuckle. "Harper, we know your healing nature. We would not come to you injured or bloody. You'd take one look, start fussing over us, and we would never get you between us in bed." He squeezed my bottom with his hand, the message unmistakable. "We won't wait to claim you, Harper."

I heard what he wasn't saying, that they would bite me soon, but that wasn't what I focused on. "You mean you came back injured and went to the med unit to be healed so I wouldn't worry?"

Styx rolled his eyes. I'd never seen him do it before and I had to assume I was the only one who could frustrate him like this. Or he'd picked up the very human body language from me. Seeing an alien warrior mimic the motion made me grin.

"Harper," he growled again.

Blade released my hand, came around and pressed into me from behind. "We were not injured, mate. We promised to come back to you. Did you doubt us?"

I turned my head to look at Blade over my shoulder, but instead he kissed me. His lips were hot, firm and eager. It seemed he didn't really want an answer.

"You are mine, Harper," Styx said. "I gave you a choice. You could have refused us. You could have gone back to the Coalition. You chose to submit. Willingly. I am done waiting, mate. The bite will make you mine forever. I am not human. There are no second chances."

I heard his words as Blade's mouth was on mine, his tongue delving, learning me once again. When Blade lifted his head, he held my gaze. "Forever, Harper." I nodded. To the kiss, to Styx's words, to Blade's promise. To everything.

"Willingly," I repeated, breathlessly. "I wanted you before you went with Doctor Mersan."

Styx's voice was quiet, calm, but brooked no argument. "We heard the truth in your words, wanted you with a desperation you can't imagine. My balls ache with the need to claim you. But we would not be deterred from finishing the Kronos traitors. They stood in the way of more than us being together. They would have brought down all Rogue 5."

His voice carried the tone of authority, that of the leader of Styx. While I saw the heat in his eyes that was solely for me, I knew, deep down, that if I wanted Styx, if I loved him as he was, I couldn't stifle his need to be in control. It was who he was at the core. And if I were to be the mate of the Styx leader, I had to understand that Rogue 5 would be his mistress. The names inked into his flesh a weight he would always carry, that I would be expected to help him bear.

I was fine with that. I would allow him to be the leader he was born to be, and he, in return, would allow me to do what was in my heart, what was in my nature. To help others. He would not deny me that, and Blade would be beside me to keep me safe as I healed those in need. Like at the mating feast, I'd healed Kronos who'd tried to kill all of us, but he'd watched over me as I did. Perhaps that was why we were perfect for each other. We fed each other's needs, and in this instance, I didn't mean sexually. I was someone Blade could protect, Styx could be bossy and dominant with —and I did mean sexually. And I would be there to heal them, to soften their heavy burdens of running the legion. The dynamic worked.

We worked.

"They also were a danger to you. The rogue Kronos," Blade added.

His pale hair was long down his back, not pulled back as usual. Neither appeared to have come from a battle. They were clean, their uniforms crisp. Either it was a tame fight they'd gone off to or they really had returned and cleaned up before coming to me. I had to wonder if they had been injured and wouldn't tell me. That was taking the whole *protective* thing a little too far. I would find out the truth, but not now. I knew which battles to pick, too.

"And now?" I asked, picking up on the word "were" in Blade's statement. They would not be standing before me, heat in Styx's eyes and the hard press of their cocks against me if it wasn't over.

If I wasn't safe.

If it wasn't time for them to bite me, claim me, make me theirs.

Maybe being whole and clean was a good thing. Nothing stood in our way—just as Styx had said—of being together. Not even the time it took to bathe. I was quickly becoming overheated. Both their bodies were so warm pressed against me. And the kisses. God, I was going to burst into flames once they got me in bed. My nipples pebbled against Styx's chest, my pussy ached, and my panties were ruined. And we were still fully clothed.

Ivar cleared his throat, prompting me to his presence, and Scribe's.

Holy crap. I was plastered between my men, and I'd *completely* forgotten their presence.

Styx inclined his chin and thanked them. I didn't look. I didn't want to see laughter or annoyance or any other emotion in either of the men's eyes. I was mortified, and that was enough.

However, out of the corner of my eye, I saw them offer a deferential nod, then exit the room. Their job was done. I was safe, and their protection was no longer required.

"And now we will continue to protect you and dominate you," Blade responded, flexing his hips which slid his cock with exquisite friction up the seam of my ass, prompting me to what he was most likely going to do soon enough. I was a little embarrassed by what Ivar and Scribe had overheard, but Blade wasn't. Nope. I had to let it go, because while Blade and Styx had said they didn't share any part of me, I would have to get used to them staking their claim in front of others. If that meant heated looks, kisses, carnal touches, then they wouldn't be denied.

And I had no interest in denying them anything. I clenched my inner walls at the thought and squirmed in Styx's hold. "I'm yours, mates. Please. Take me. Bite me. You can have anything. Anything you want." It was more than a promise, it was surrender. Complete. Total. I gave them everything.

Styx growled, spun me about and carried me out of the room. He only lowered me to my feet before them when we were alone in his quarters, in front of his big bed. "Strip, mate. I have been longing to see your soft skin."

Styx's command made me shiver. While they hadn't held their true selves back when we'd been in the back hallway of the canteen on Zenith, we'd been in a not-so-private place. And at the mating feast, they'd made me come on their fingers with a ruthless precision and a bold dominance, but they'd still held back because we'd again been in a hallway, in a semi-public place. Even when they'd fucked me for the first time, knowing I was their mate, they'd held back because their true nature as Hyperion had been to bite me. They'd had to stifle that innate need because I hadn't been ready.

I hadn't begged.

While they'd been wild and bold, calculating and so dang dominant they'd made me come on command, I hadn't seen the real Styx or Blade.

Now I could. I would. No, I *did*, with just the word "strip".

My entire body shivered, grew shaky with anticipation, at what might come next.

I'd never imagined I'd want someone like Styx who gave orders that were meant to be followed, not questioned. Then again, I'd never been aroused as I was with them. Orgasms? Yeah, never like this. Maybe it had taken a trip halfway across the universe to discover I was into kink.

Into two men at once. Dominance. Whatever else they had in mind.

I wanted it all.

So when they stood before me with fierce gazes and hard cocks pressing against their black pants, I didn't argue.

I stripped. Naked. As fast as my fingers could fly over the fabric.

Yeah, my fingers shook, but it wasn't in fear. It was with anticipation. I wasn't the only impatient one. Waiting for them to return had been horrible. But now...I'd forgotten about everything but them. This. Gods, I was going to come just taking off my clothes. It was as if they had pheromones pumping off them.

Two big, fierce, brooding, crazy aliens were standing before me, their eyes raking over every inch of my body.

They wanted me with a need and intensity I'd never known existed.

I tossed the black shirt over my head. I looked down, saw my hard nipples through my thin bra. They saw them too, and Blade's hands clenched into fists as Styx groaned. He rubbed his cock through his pants as if it hurt him.

Feeling empowered, I toed off my boots and pulled off the rest of my clothes. Knowing these two big, brawny and controlling men were reduced to cock rubbing and clenched fists made feel like I was the one who led them. Perhaps around by their blue balls.

Some of my insecurities flared to life when they stood there unmoving, still as statues and just stared at my nakedness. Even with the soft lighting in his bedroom, I was sure they could see every imperfection, the slight dimpling on my hips which no exercise would make go away. My boobs, while I was proud of them, hadn't defied gravity. Then there was my—

"So beautiful," Blade murmured, running his tongue along his teeth.

"Do you know why we're standing here, not touching you?" Styx asked.

I placed my hands on the sides of my hips to cover myself, even a little bit. "I thought maybe it was because—"

Styx sliced his hand through the air. "I know what you're going to say and I'm cutting you off. If you mention any kind of imperfection on your body, you'll be over my knee with a red ass."

He meant it. My cheeks flushed at them knowing me so well.

"We're standing here trying to calm down enough not to

bite you right now. To pull out our cocks and claim you with two quick thrusts and our sharp teeth."

My mouth fell open at his very honest words. I knew they were attracted. Eager, even.

They looked at each other for a second, then back at me. Grinned.

"Oh."

They had fangs. Like vampires. Their incisors were long and pointed and dangerous looking. I froze, like a deer in the headlights. Prey. I was prey.

I wanted to be caught.

A slight sheen built on the tip of Styx's fang, and I stared, trying to figure out what I was seeing.

"Serum," he said, as if reading my mind. "Once that's in your flesh, you're mine."

"And mine," Blade added, running his tongue over his teeth again.

"Arousal, desire, need. All of it will swirl together in the most incredible pleasure you've ever imagined. And that's just the first orgasm. From then on, you'll be needy, achy, begging for us."

I was wet, and when Styx took a deep breath, his pale green eyes went dark. He picked up the scent of my arousal and groaned. If they looked down, they'd see it coating my pussy.

"I could live between your thighs. My mouth on you for hours," he continued.

I wiggled my hips at the thought. They were both quite good at oral and had done it as foreplay every time they'd fucked me. And they weren't quick about it either, lingering on me until I came for them several times. Only then would they fuck me, saying they needed me nice and soft and swollen, nice and wet for their big cocks. The tally of orgasms was skewed in my favor. It wasn't even close.

"You want my mouth on you?" Blade asked, opening his pants and pulling out his cock. "You want this?"

I stared at him, his hand gripping the base firmly, the thick vein pulsing up the whole length. The tip was flared, a ruddy red and fluid seeped from the narrow slit. My mouth watered to get a taste of him.

I could only nod.

"Where do you want it, mate?" Blade's gaze wandered over me, and he was grinning again.

I opened my mouth to respond, but words? What the hell was a word? I had none. Images flooded my mind. Images and memory and sensation. Hands. Mouths. My hot, wet pussy feeling stretched and pulsing with release. The smell of their skin. Heat of their hands. Being caught in the center of the maelstrom that was them. "Everywhere." Hands. Mouths. Cocks. I was going to jump them if they didn't move soon. "Now."

Styx's eyes darkened with pleasure at my eagerness, his focus absolute. "Turn around. Slowly." As if he could read my mind, Styx continued, "Not everywhere. Pussy and ass while we bite you."

"Okay," I completed my turn. They hadn't moved closer, but as least Styx was taking off his clothes. When he was fully naked, it was my turn to be frozen in place. He was so gorgeous. Tall and broad, muscled and hard. The tattoos were a visible reminder of his role, of his honor. My name on him only made me wetter knowing I belonged to him. And the piercings...I shouldn't even think about the piercings or I'd come.

My hands on my hips, I decided, could be put to much

better use. I closed my eyes, tilted my head back and slid them over my skin in a sensual glide, touching myself the way I wanted them to touch me. I moved one hand to my breast and pinched the nipple until it pebbled into a hard peak. The other I slid lower, dipping between the wet folds of my pussy.

Eyes open just enough to watch their reactions, I knew I had them when I saw Blade raise a trembling hand to his hair, his gaze darting to Styx in question? For permission? Styx's chest was heaving.

"Fuck your pussy with your finger, mate. Slide it in deep."

I did as he commanded, made sure to moan softly as I rubbed over my clit.

In the blink of an eye, Styx had his hands around my waist and tossed me onto the bed in a half circle so I came up facing him. When I pulled myself up onto my knees, I realized he liked to do that, to put me right where he wanted me. I loved that he didn't treat me like spun glass. I wasn't fragile, and these two better not hold back any longer. I wanted rough. Wild. Crazy. Dirty. I wanted their cocks, their fangs. Everything.

Blade was still stripping as Styx put one knee on the bed and pulled me to him, kissing me. His lips were firm, skilled, but I didn't engage.

I pulled back, curious. I lifted my fingers to his mouth, traced the fang there with my fingertip. "Will it hurt?" I asked. I didn't care, either way, but I wanted to know. I didn't mind a bite of pain mixed with my pleasure, but I didn't want to be surprised. I was breathing hard even though we hadn't done much of anything yet.

Styx smiled, showed me the fangs were gone. "I have been told the pleasure overrides the pain."

"You haven't bitten anyone before, right?" I couldn't resist putting my hands on him, sliding my palms over his hard muscles, the names on his skin, the piercings. "Have you been bitten?" A hot burn of jealousy made me want to make claws with my fingers and rip any Rogue 5 female's eyes out for even looking at my mates. The thought of something so intimate as being between them and their fangs imbedded in another woman's flesh made me irrational. The crazy feeling was swift to overwhelm me, yet I couldn't help it. We'd been through so much, and I was beyond ready to really belong to them. Permanently and in a way that proudly proved that fact to anyone who saw the scars I would bear the rest of my life.

They both shook their heads, eyed my neck. "A mating bite is forever, mate. Sacred. We only ever give our bite to one female."

"So you're biting virgins?" I asked, raising an eyebrow and fighting back a laugh at my own bad joke. But the humor helped. I was about to be double-fucked and bitten and injected by some kind of animalistic mating serum by two huge, warrior aliens.

Blade made a strange chuffing sound, and I looked to him. He grinned, and I saw the sharp teeth. "We've been waiting for you to come to us from half a universe away. Think about that. How almost impossible that is. We're yours, mate. You will be our first—and last." He took a step closer. "As for virgins, did you like it when I fucked your ass with my big cock?" He grabbed said cock at the base and stroked it. Yeah, they were *very* skilled.

I clenched down, remembering the thick feel of him, the

way he'd been patient yet persistent as he'd taken me there. Deep, lighting me up so I'd come so intensely I'd almost blacked out.

"Yes," I murmured, reaching for him. When Blade stepped close enough, I ran my fingertips over the crown of his cock, felt the smear of wetness.

"For the last time, Harper. Do you accept us as your mates knowing that we will claim you completely, that you'll bear our marks upon your skin for all to see? For all to know who you belong to. Who protects you?" He leaned into my touch, and I wrapped my hand around him the best I could, pumping his hard length with my fist. He moaned, but he kept talking. "If anyone hurts you, Harper. I will kill him. I will fucking kill him."

Blade's words were like personal vows as his hands dropped to my waist and his eyes closed. There would be no turning back after this. He was giving me one last chance to say no. To walk away—although I didn't think I'd get far. I'd be wooed, courted Rogue 5-style if I wasn't ready. They'd keep at it until I said yes, no matter how long it took.

I studied Blade, all pale hair and sharp edges—not including his teeth. Then I took in Styx, all dark and rough, commanding and yet so damned patient. Both had swoonworthy bodies. Big, broad, muscled. The tattoos though, showed that they cared, that they protected and guided everyone listed on their skin. Including me. I couldn't miss my name on both their chests. It was also the piercings, the small bars that went through their nipples. I'd played with them with my fingers, flicked them with my tongue and did the same now with Styx's. They may not have bitten me, but they'd said again and again I was theirs. That I was their mate. And this physical proof of it was exposed proudly to me and anyone who might see it.

Even without the bites, they'd already claimed me. I was already theirs. They were just waiting for me to accept them as mine.

They were so brave, so strong; it was difficult for me to remember they had feelings, that I was probably the one person who could cut them ruthlessly. The only person who could truly wound them.

But I didn't want that. No. I wanted their cocks, the ones that stood erect and proud, curved up toward their navels and bobbing at me. Every part of them, from their alpha male protectiveness to their rocking bodies, was mine.

They were tightly coiled, ready to spring into action, to claim me. I just had to say the one word that would unleash them. And bring about their darkest desires, their deepest need to make me theirs. To take me at the same time, one deep in my pussy, the other in my ass. Their heads on either side of mine, fangs embedded in my flesh. And that serum, I couldn't wait for it.

I took a deep breath, let it out. This was the moment, the moment that changed my life forever. And yet, I had no doubts. No regrets.

"Bite me. Make me yours. I want you. I want you both."

All patience was gone. While their muscles relaxed—had they been worried I'd say no?—they didn't go slowly. In fact, they moved quickly, flipping and turning me around so Styx was sitting on the edge of the bed, and I was on his lap, his cock pressed between our bellies.

"Aren't we...um, going to lie down?" I asked, thinking of how they'd take me together. I'd seen a few pornos, but not double penetration. There was some logistics involved.

Aiming. Depth. Body parts in the way. I was flexible, but I was no gymnast. I actually had no idea how they were going to do this. But based on the way they talked, that they'd been dreaming of this, I was sure they knew what they were doing. When Styx's hands came up and cupped my breasts, plucked my nipples, I gave everything over to them. Shut my brain down and just let myself *feel*. So damn good.

Looking over my shoulder, I saw Blade lower to one knee on the floor behind me, his silver hair catching the light. I wanted to run my fingers through it, but it seemed they had other plans.

"Take me into that tight pussy," Styx said, using his fingertips to turn my face back to his. He shifted his hips, sliding his cock between us. He hissed. "We'll take care of you."

I knew that, but I loved hearing it. However they were going to claim me together, they had a plan. I would trust in them that they'd make it good. They had every time so far.

Styx lowered a hand to my hip, helped me come up onto my knees and aligned his cock to my entrance. He slipped right into the notch because I was so wet. Lowering myself, I slowly stretched open around him, taking the broad head, then the thick root deeper and deeper. I watched Styx, saw the need there. Knew he liked being inside me. I didn't stop until I sat upon his thighs once again, this time fully impaled on him.

I groaned; Styx growled. It felt so good, I rippled around him. "I need to move."

I couldn't remain still. I needed the friction, the slide of his hard flesh over every single nerve ending inside me. My g-spot—which I'd never known existed until their cocks—

flared and pushed me to the brink with every pass of his cock.

I put my hands on Styx's shoulders, lifting and lowering myself as he thrust his hips up. I rode him, lost in the feel of it until Blade's finger brushed over my back entrance.

It was slick and cool with lube and easily pressed into me. I had no idea where the lube came from, but it wasn't time to think of logistics. It wasn't time to think of anything. I slowed my hips, allowing Blade to gain entrance—he'd been very diligent in preparing me for this that I knew how to relax, to breathe out when he wanted in. I liked it. Craved it. It burned, yes. The pressure, the odd feeling of being open was...different. But my body didn't care. No. It liked it. Loved it. Craved the way the nerve endings in my ass lit up with his touch. He'd fucked me there before, his cock stretching me impossibly open, but it had been just him. Nothing in my pussy. Just one of them.

I wanted more this time. Ached for it.

While Blade was thick and stretched my ass so unbelievably wide, when Styx had taken me there, he'd gone deeper, filled me in a way no one ever had.

It seemed for the claiming, it would be Blade in my ass, Styx in my pussy.

Styx lifted one hand and buried his fist in my hair. He angled my head and took my mouth, sliding his tongue in and out of me as Blade worked me with his finger and Styx's cock stretched me wide. I couldn't think, couldn't track the sensations as Styx slid his other hand to the small of my back and moved my body into an arch so my clit rubbed his body with each shift and tilt of my hips.

Fast and faster Blade fucked me, stretching me for his

cock as Styx fucked me slow and deep, the orgasm building as he led me down the path he wanted me to follow.

I gave him complete control, let them mold me, fill me. Fuck me.

The first orgasm built slowly, rising from inside me like a dormant volcano, the pressure building and building until I lost control.

Styx held me still, arm locked like a steel bar around my back as he pushed my hips down, my legs splayed wider, deeper. Blade's fingers worked my ass and his free hand slid between my chest and Styx's to grab my nipple, pinch and tug and send jolts of electricity to my core as my pussy spasmed, my toes curled. I didn't recognize the sound that came out of my throat. Blade slowly added another finger and another until he was satisfied I was stretched open enough for his cock. Only then did he pull out.

I moaned, feeling empty with just Styx in me. Blade chuckled, pressed a kiss to my sweaty shoulder. "Just a minute, mate. I'll be in you soon enough."

He was good on his word, for once he'd coated his cock with lube, I felt the tip of it press against my prepared entrance. Styx held me by the hips, not moving, remaining completely inside me, the head of his cock pressing deep against my womb where he'd plant his seed. Fill me with *him*. Give me everything. His cum was mine. His cock was mine. His body was mine.

"Mine. You're mine. You're both mine." The whisper was my vow to them, my pledge. My turn to tell them exactly what I expected. I was hot, my pulse pounding. My entire body pliant, aroused. Needy.

Blade put a hand on my shoulder, pushed me forward so

I pressed against Styx's chest. I felt the hard bars of his piercings brush against my sensitive nipples.

Sweat dripped from Styx's brow, and I licked his jaw, tasted the salty flavor of his skin. I whimpered when Blade pressed further, my body giving up the natural resistance to keep him out and he popped inside.

He held still, the broad head just settled within me. He leaned forward, kissing my shoulder. "I love your tight ass, mate," he breathed as he pushed in slightly.

"Oh my god," I murmured. I was so full, and Blade hadn't even gone into me very much yet. To say being fucked by two guys at once was intense was an understatement.

It was powerful in that I was between them, and I was submitting to them both. Their dominance was powerful. I could do nothing but let them in. Sure, I could say stop and they'd pull out immediately, but my submission was based on that knowledge. I gave over to them. To the feel of them in me.

Together.

My body burned. Hummed. Ached. Stretched. Pulsed. I was everything at once. I was theirs.

Blade slid in a little further, then retreated, fucking me slowly and carefully all the while Styx remained still. "I'm going to come," I said, kissing up Styx's neck, squirming, trying to rub my clit against him.

It was too much. I couldn't hold back the way they made me feel. I'd come once, and it was as if that warm-up pleasure had made me sensitive, easy to come again. Or it was them.

"Not yet," Styx breathed. "Let Blade in all the way. Good.

More. Yes, I can feel him getting deeper and deeper. I can feel you clenching our cocks. Hold off the orgasm."

"Why?" I whined, resistance almost impossible. I was quivering with the need to come, but Styx's words held me just at the edge. I wanted to please them.

"Because we will come with you. We will bite you as we give you our seed, and the pleasure you receive from us will be unlike anything you've ever felt."

My fingers clenched Styx's biceps as Blade pressed into me. "Almost there."

Styx fell back on the bed and pulled me with him. I felt Blade come up off his knee and to his feet, his hand pressing the bed down by my head. I felt his torso press against my back as he thrust deep one last time. He was fully seated, and they were both so deep I didn't know where I stopped and they began.

They both pulled out, pushed back in, filling me so full, fucked me slow and so, so deep.

I pressed my forehead to Styx's chest and trembled. Whimpered. I wasn't me. I was something else. Lost. Drowning in heat. In lust. In pleasure.

"It's time, mate," Styx growled, leaning up, his abs going taut as he kissed down my neck.

Blade's head came to my other shoulder, nipped it with his teeth and then settled where he would bite me. He kissed the tender spot as he pulled back and filled me again.

"Yes, please! I need to—"

I didn't get to finish the sentence.

They bit me, their mouths over the base of my neck on either side. I felt their lips open, the sharpness of their fangs as they pierced my flesh.

In one hot, bright moment, the pain was so intense I

screamed. In the next instant, the pain was gone, morphed into pleasure. Pleasure so intense I didn't clench on them. I didn't scream. I didn't breathe. I was captured. There was no Harper. I was part of them. Connected. I was theirs. Found. Their bodies my anchor in a storm of sensation so strong I lost track of myself.

I didn't know how to control my body. My nipples ached, throbbed. My pussy gushed my arousal, signaling to Styx that he was welcome within, that I wanted him as deep as possible.

I felt their seed filling me, their bodies taut. They groaned with their teeth still latched to me. Their cocks pulsed with their own pleasure, pumping into me.

I was nothing. I was everything. I felt the serum seep into my bloodstream, into my bones. They were right; I was going to be a horny mate if this was how they would make me feel from now on.

I caught my breath as if I'd come up from beneath the ocean, a huge gasp and then a scream of pleasure. "Yes!" I cried. I couldn't move. Pinned between them, skewered on their cocks, caught on their fangs, I was trapped. I was theirs. There was nowhere else in the universe I wanted to be as my body rippled. The orgasm took me like a tidal wave, rolling through every muscle, every cell alive with pleasure I'd never felt before. It was terrifying and exquisite, dangerous, and so addictive I knew I'd never get enough.

My body arched and writhed as the orgasm pulled me under like a riptide pulling me out to sea. Ruled me. Made me mindless.

When it was over, they lifted their heads, licked my bite marks with their bloody tongues. I thought they would pull out. That we were done.

I was wrong. Their cocks remained hard. They'd only slowed the pace of the fucking while their own release, their bite overwhelmed them.

"Good?" Styx asked, his voice ragged.

I lifted my head, looked down at him. He frowned slightly, and I smiled. Deliriously. "Amazing."

He grinned then.

Blade pressed up to his hand again, slid the other one down my spine.

"You've made mates of us, Harper. Now it's time to fuck."

He began to move within me again, slowly, but his seed eased the way better than the lube.

"Don't you have to rest?"

Styx had a wicked gleam in his eyes.

"Does it seem like our cocks aren't ready for you?"

"Um, no."

Blade kissed my neck, kept moving within me. "Get ready, mate. The only way we'll stop is when you pass out from pleasure."

My mouth fell open, waited for Styx to contradict Blade. He didn't.

"Again," Styx said instead. "And again."

They didn't stop fucking me. Not for the rest of the day. In ways I never imagined. I came again and again, each time better than the last. I was insatiable. I was horny. Everything they said was true. It was perfect. *They* were perfect.

I was theirs, and they proved it for me.

Until, just as Blade had said, they stopped making love to me for a few seconds, and I passed out from exhaustion.

I fell asleep safe. Warm. Wrung out. Protected.

Happy. Loved. They were mine now. Mine.

Forever.

EPILOGUE

*S*tyx, *Two Weeks Later*

"Follow me." Silver led the way down a corridor from my private quarters with Blade and Harper to a large banquet room. Harper walked between us, Blade and I on either side.

Each holding one of her hands.

This was the new normal, our mate safe and protected. Between us. Soothing our savage instincts with softness and smiles and surrender in bed.

Not just surrender. Submission. She gave over to our possession beautifully and now bore our marks. Just seeing them made me hard.

We'd been wild when we returned from our routing of the Kronos traitors. Animalistic in our need to claim her, make sure she was safe and real and ours.

But our ferocity had not scared her. The opposite, in

fact. The wilder we were, the wetter her pussy, the harder she wanted to fuck. Deeper. Just...more.

A fact that I often took advantage of.

The footage from the Kronos cargo ship had been seen by everyone on Rogue 5. Silver, the sneaky female, had kept her recording device on when we went into the command deck. She'd edited the content to show me ripping out the Kronos soldier's throat, my warning, and then an image of Blade ripping the enforcer's head off as I stood by with a look of cold disinterest on my face.

It had the desired effect across the moon base.

Styx was more powerful than ever. Kronos legion was quiet, licking their wounds and watching their backs.

The other legion leaders helped me keep tabs on them, keeping them in check and would do so for the foreseeable future.

There were no Prillon warriors, no Atlans, no Doctor Mersan on Silver's video. She was smart. She knew that Styx legion needed to be perceived as vicious. Merciless. Strong.

And Harper?

We kept the footage from her. She knew she was mated to rogues, but I wanted her protected from the ruthlessness that came with my leadership. I would not have her witness to such darkness. It was a difficult task, but everyone knew she had to be protected. Perhaps she herself knew this and didn't fight us on it. Avoided the footage even.

We'd claimed her, and she glowed. The serum certainly made her eager for us, but it hadn't been necessary. She'd been eager from the first moment I saw her in that canteen on Zenith. Our people loved her. After her selfless service at the mating feast, where she'd saved the lives of enforcers and captains from the other legions as tirelessly as she'd helped Styx, she'd become something of a celebrity.

Everyone loved my mate. Everyone wanted her. A touch. A hello. A kiss for their little ones. A smile.

While I garnered respect, she got their affection. I didn't know anyone on the moon belt who *liked* me.

It was driving me fucking insane. I knew the political gift this was, the leverage I would have over the other legions, the pull I'd have with their people. I knew, and still I hated sharing her.

We were protective and possessive assholes.

Blade was worse. He was her shadow, ever on the lookout for an attack.

But that fierce protectiveness was the only reason I could breathe when she was out of sight. I knew when she was not with me, she was with him.

Gods. Who knew falling in love would be such a fucking mess?

Silver walked slowly, her uniform crisp, new. Her hair was in an elaborate braid I'd rarely seen her bother with.

"What's going on, little sister?" Blade's voice was curious, but content. He smiled more now that we had Harper. Hell, so did I.

"It's a surprise. Just shut up and play along."

Play along? I never did that. I had to know what was happening. Be prepared. Plan. Lead.

"I don't like surprises, Silver." My voice was neither content nor curious, but irritated. She'd interrupted us when we'd been in bed. Harper splayed over my chest, skin to skin. Heart to heart. Cock settled deep inside her, my seed slipping out because there was always too much for her tight channel. My favorite way to hold her. Silver's knock on the door cost me precious moments with my mate.

As she continued down the corridor, Silver laughed and opened the door to the largest gathering room we had in Styx territory.

We followed her in and Harper's eyes went wide. My throat grew thick, achy. So heavy I knew I would not be able to speak. I squeezed Harper's hand.

"By the gods." Blade's awed tone said it all.

The entire legion was gathered. Three thousand strong. Children ran around, laughing and screaming and playing like this was the annual festival of gifts. They didn't know the weight of the moment, but they would someday.

The crowd parted for us as we passed, creating a clear path to a raised platform where Scribe stood with Khon, Cormac and Ivar.

"Silver?" Her name was a question, to which she laughed and ignored me.

What the fuck was going on here? I sensed no danger, only heavy emotion.

We followed Silver up onto the stage and everyone just... stopped. Even the babies seemed to be holding their breaths. The silence was so heavy Scribe didn't even need to raise his voice to be heard.

"Welcome Styx legion."

They erupted in loud cheers, which lasted until Scribe raised his hand to silence them.

"We have gathered to honor our new lady and her mates. Our blood. Our heart. Our strength."

Cheers. Louder. The room seemed to rock with the sound and Harper's chest rose and fell in rapid waves, her hand choking the blood from mine in her tight grip.

While she might heal, she hated to be the center of attention.

Blade leaned around her to look at me. "Do you know what the fuck is going on?"

I shook my head and scanned the screaming crowd. It was not often we saw everyone so damned happy. "No fucking idea."

"Shut up, both of you." Harper's smile was wobbly and her eyes filled with tears. She knew. Damn female intuition.

Blade's confusion turned to alpha protection mode when he saw her crying. "What is wrong? Are you hurt? Why are you crying?" His voice boomed, and he pulled her to him, checking her over.

She laughed and pushed him away. We both relaxed. "You two can be really dense."

"Dense? What does that mean?" I asked. Sometimes, her Earth vernacular required more translation than the NPUs could provide.

Scribe stepped to the side and swept his hand out toward our enforcers, who had moved and organized at the front. They stepped forward and stripped their shirts from their bodies. The men stood bare chested and Silver remained covered in only a thin band that contained her breasts for battle.

Styx legion roared approval, and I felt my body go numb. For the first time, I was caught by surprise and had no idea what to do about it.

This was impossible. No outsider had ever—no.

Silver stepped up first and knelt with her bare shoulder before Scribe. "Her name is Harper, Scribe. And she is mine."

The room was tense as Scribe leaned down and inked

Harper's name into Silver's flesh. The buzz from the needle was the only sound that filled the room.

Cormac, Ivar and Khon followed suit and Harper swayed between us. We closed in, surrounded her with our heat and strength, our love as the time dragged on.

My enforcers were followed by the captains.

They were followed by the civilian leaders of every sector.

My enforcers stood at attention in respect until the final ink was placed. When the last bit of ink was finished, we turned to face the legion. They kneeled, every man and woman pulling the neck of their shirt to the side to reveal the freshly healed placement of their new marks. Harper's name had been added to everyone, the dedication and declaration of the entire Styx legion as one. She was our mate, but she belonged to our people as well.

Harper broke free from our hold and walked toward Scribe, wiping tears from her eyes.

She pulled her own shirt from her head and knelt at his feet.

Without thought, I moved to block her, to shield her from view of everyone. She wore just a bra and while it was black and plain, she was sharing more skin than I wanted. Her body was for my eyes—and Blade's—only. Grabbing the shirt from her fingers, I covered her with it, although it didn't do much good.

She ignored my efforts and said, "I claim them all."

The responding sound that came from the gathering now made the previous roar sound like a baby's weak wailings.

Blade leaped forward as Scribe raised the needle to her flesh, stopping him by holding his wrist. "No!" He turned to me, panic in his eyes at the pain Harper would endure.

Harper's green gaze lifted to mine, the love and devotion there humbled me, and I dropped to kneel before her.

"You're serious about this?" I asked her. My voice was quiet, but no one could hear.

She nodded. "I'm sure."

I looked at the scars on either side of her neck. They'd healed well, only slightly pink still in contrast to her pale skin. But no one would question her loyalty with those marks. The double bites. That wasn't enough for her. She wanted more. She wanted to be like us. I kept a hand on her back, holding the shirt over her bare skin, offering a little bit of modesty.

While she might not be modest, I was for her.

Blade loomed over both of us, blocking out the legion. He nodded once.

I looked to Harper who waited. She was willing to accept my answer, but it was probably because she knew I would give in. She knew this was important to the people. To her. Surprisingly, even to me.

"One name should suffice, Scribe," I said.

He grinned, tilted his head slightly. "I agree."

While I kept my mate as covered as possible and Blade remained our protective eyes, "Styx" was inked into our mate's flesh. Blade placed a steadying hand on her bare shoulder as the needle pierced her skin over and over.

I watched her face closely for any signs of discomfort. Half my body was covered in ink; I knew how it felt, but I would stop it if it were too much for Harper. While her cheeks colored and she breathed steadily through parted lips, she remained motionless. Stoic.

A young one crawled out of her mother's arms and onto the stage. She was a babe, not yet able to walk, but she made her way to my mate and crawled into her lap.

Everyone went silent, waiting to see what my mate would do.

I already knew.

When Harper smiled down at the babe and kissed her on one soft, tiny cheek, the room roared back to life.

Harper held the child as the mark of our legion was inked into her flesh, right above her heart.

She looked out over the crowd, up at Blade, down at the babe in her arms, then up at me.

"I want one of these," she said. "And you're going to give it to me."

My heart nearly ruptured. "Bossy, aren't you?"

"You haven't figured that out by now?"

I grinned. My cock pressed painfully against my uniform pants at the thought of filling her with our seed, it taking root and Harper swelling with our child. A little girl, with her pretty hair and green eyes. Or a boy, rough and tumble, but generous and caring, too. A mixture of Harper and her mates.

"Yes."

"Yes, you've figured it out?"

"Yes, to the baby."

I glanced at Blade. "You could be with child now," he reminded.

Shaking her head, our mate looked sad. "No, Coalition fighters and volunteers all have birth control. Mine is to last until the end of my two years."

She brushed her cheek over the top of the baby's soft head, then handed her back to her mother. Scribe stood, his work done, and I turned her shoulders to face me, so I could see my name over her breast.

I groaned at the sight.

Blade squatted down on his haunches. "Once we are finished here, we will go to the med unit and reverse it." Ever the protector. We didn't want her upset, even in this. I should laugh. Two rogue leaders brought to their knees by a woman from Earth.

"Think of all the times we fucked as practice," I added.

She smiled then, brilliantly, but her hand came up to her reddened flesh. I knew she would not want a ReGen wand on the tender skin now, but as soon as we were away from the legion and in the med unit, we would see her fully healed. Especially if we were going to put a baby in her.

"I love you, you know. I love you both."

I pulled her into my arms, and I kissed her. Hard. Deep. Claiming her in front of the entire legion as she shifted to wrap her arms around my neck.

When she moaned and clung to me, I let her come up for air. The legion yelled and clapped and whistled their approval as Blade moved closer.

"I love you, Harper."

Blade echoed my words and we turned to face our people.

Everyone had seen my name, the legion's name, be inked on her skin. That was enough. They didn't have to ogle. I would. Blade would. Gods, we'd fuck her so we could see the mark, kiss it, as we drove into her, knowing she was ours just as much by that as the scars on her neck.

Silver bowed low to our mate and spoke for everyone in the room. "Welcome home."

The words were repeated by all. There was nothing else

to do. They'd shown their allegiance and Harper had given hers in return. It was time to get on with living, for now, in peace. If our mate wanted a baby, it was our job to give it to her. Starting now. I stood, lifting Harper with me as I did so, tossing her over my shoulder. The crowd parted for me and Blade as I carried a surprised mate out of the room—to much applause—and to the med unit.

Within, the doctors looked up. Surprised. Worried.

"My mate wants a baby." I placed a hand on her shoulder. Blade moved up, did the same with the other. "Make her fertile, and we will do the rest."

With pink cheeks, she cried my name and looked up at me. "Bossy, much?"

I grinned. "With you? Absolutely. Get on with it, doctor," I ordered.

One came up with a wand, one I'd never seen before.

"Yes, doctor," Blade added. "We have a mate to fuck. A baby to make."

"There's a problem," the doctor said. Tilting her head to the side, she looked at Harper.

I pulled my mate into my arms, held her tight. "A problem? Is she sick? Fix her. Heal her."

The doctor laughed. In that moment, I wanted to rip her head from her shoulders. Didn't she know I was in a panic?

"Styx," she said, trying to calm my panic.

Out of the corner of my eye, I saw Blade's body go rigid.

"Styx," she repeated. She waited patiently as my brain returned to focusing on her instead of all the possibilities that could be harming our mate.

"I can't make her fertile."

My heart skipped a beat, not realizing how painful those words were. I had no idea I wanted a child until now. And then have it yanked from me. Gods, Harper would be crushed. She would—

"I can't make her fertile because she already is. She's pregnant."

Harper gasped, her hands dropping to her flat stomach.

"What?" All three of us said the word at the same time.

The doctor smiled, looked down at her wand. "It's very early, but this sensor is accurate. You, mate of leader Styx, are pregnant. Congratulations."

"But, but..." Harper went lax in my hold. "I was given birth control on Earth before I was transported. It was to last over two years."

The doctor just shrugged. "I can run more tests, but no alarms come up from the basic readings. You are healthy. Come see me in a few weeks, or if you have any concerns."

I was panicking. My heart rate was higher than during battle. My mate was safe. She wasn't sick, and yet I was afraid. "I carried her over my shoulder."

"I was rough when I fucked her earlier," Blade added.

The doctor laughed. "While I don't recommend carrying her over your shoulder for long, you have not harmed the baby. And as for intercourse, I assure you, there are no restrictions."

I looked to Blade over Harper's head. A grin spread across his face. "A father."

"Yes," I replied. I tilted Harper's chin up, kissed her gently.

"Oh no, you're not going to go all gentle on me now, are you? The doctor just said there are no restrictions."

Blade scooped Harper up and carried her out of the med unit, calling his thanks over his shoulder as he went.

I followed, ensuring he didn't drop her. I was being an

idiot, but our mate was carrying our child. We'd put it there. All at once I felt virile. My cock pulsed, my balls ached with my very potent seed.

"Faster, Blade. We have a mate to fuck."

Harper glanced at me over Blade's shoulder. "The baby's in there already."

"Yes, but we've been very thorough so far. It pays to continue." I was being ridiculous, but I had a feeling I'd lost my mind along with my heart.

Not only did I have to worry about Harper, but a baby too. I was doomed. I would be the only pussy-whipped leader on the moon belt.

I grinned as we walked into my quarters, and Blade gently placed her on the bed.

I didn't mind being pussy-whipped as long as it was Harper's pussy.

"Strip," I commanded.

I watched Harper's eyes go blurry with desire as she pushed down her pants, and we could see her pussy.

Yes, we were whipped and we'd spend the rest of our lives enjoying every moment.

———

Ready for more? Read Claimed By The Vikens next!
The only thing former Coalition warriors Calder, Zed and Axon have in common are long years spent battling the Hive, and their eagerness to claim their personal reward—their own Interstellar Bride.

When news arrives on Viken that each of the warriors has

been matched, they gather at the transport station only to receive two unwelcome surprises.

First, they are all matched to the same woman, and not one of them is inclined to share.
Second, their mate has refused them.
She won't leave Earth and transport to Viken.
Won't give any of them a chance to win her heart.
But these warriors will not back down from a challenge.
When one states his intention to travel to Earth and retrieve his mate,
the others will not allow him to make the journey alone.

Their mate will be seduced.
Claimed.
One by one,
they will tame her.
Make her their own.
May the best male win...

Click here to read Claimed By The Vikens now!

A SPECIAL THANK YOU TO MY READERS...

Want more? I've got *hidden* bonus content on my web site *exclusively* for those on my mailing list.

If you are already on my email list, you don't need to do a thing! Simply scroll to the bottom of my newsletter emails and click on the *super-secret* link.

Not a member? What are you waiting for? In addition to ALL of my bonus content (great new stuff will be added regularly) you will be the first to hear about my newest release the second it hits the stores—AND you will get a free book as a special welcome gift.

Sign up now! http://freescifiromance.com

FIND YOUR INTERSTELLAR MATCH!

YOUR mate is out there. Take the test today and discover your perfect match. Are you ready for a sexy alien mate (or two)?

VOLUNTEER NOW!

interstellarbridesprogram.com

DO YOU LOVE AUDIOBOOKS?

Grace Goodwin's books are now available as audiobooks...everywhere.

LET'S TALK SPOILER ROOM!

Interested in joining my **Sci-Fi Squad**? Meet new like-minded sci-fi romance fanatics and chat with Grace! Get excerpts, cover reveals and sneak peeks before anyone else. Be part of a private Facebook group that shares pictures and fun news! Join here:

https://www.facebook.com/groups/scifisquad/

***

Want to talk about Grace Goodwin books with others? Join the **SPOILER ROOM** and spoil away! Your GG BFFs are waiting! (And so is Grace)

Join here:

https://www.facebook.com/groups/ggspoilerroom/

GET A FREE BOOK!

JOIN MY MAILING LIST TO BE THE FIRST TO KNOW OF NEW
RELEASES, FREE BOOKS, SPECIAL PRICES AND OTHER
AUTHOR GIVEAWAYS.

http://freescifiromance.com

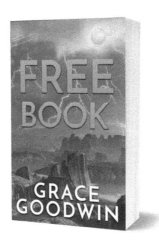

ALSO BY GRACE GOODWIN

Mated to the Cyborgs

Cyborg Seduction

Her Cyborg Beast

Cyborg Fever

Rogue Cyborg

Cyborg's Secret Baby

Her Cyborg Warriors

Interstellar Brides® Program: The Virgins

The Alien's Mate

His Virgin Mate

Claiming His Virgin

His Virgin Bride

His Virgin Princess

Interstellar Brides® Program: Ascension Saga

Ascension Saga, book 1

Ascension Saga, book 2

Ascension Saga, book 3

Trinity: Ascension Saga - Volume 1

Ascension Saga, book 4

Ascension Saga, book 5

Ascension Saga, book 6

Faith: Ascension Saga - Volume 2

Ascension Saga, book 7

Ascension Saga, book 8

Ascension Saga, book 9

Destiny: Ascension Saga - Volume 3

Other Books

Their Conquered Bride

Wild Wolf Claiming: A Howl's Romance

ABOUT GRACE

Grace Goodwin is a USA Today and international bestselling author of Sci-Fi and Paranormal romance with more than one million books sold. Grace's titles are available worldwide in multiple languages in ebook, print and audio formats. Two best friends, one left-brained, the other right-brained, make up the award-winning writing duo that is Grace Goodwin.

They are both mothers, escape room enthusiasts, avid readers and intrepid defenders of their preferred beverages. (There may or may not be an ongoing tea vs. coffee war occurring during their daily communications.) Grace loves to hear from readers!

All of Grace's books can be read as sexy, stand-alone adventures. But be careful, she likes her heroes hot and her love scenes hotter. You have been warned...

www.gracegoodwin.com
gracegoodwinauthor@gmail.com

Lightning Source UK Ltd.
Milton Keynes UK
UKHW021433030321
379713UK00008B/2164

9 781795 901598